I'm Kate Fortune—
the matriarch of the Fortune family.

My dearly departed husband, Ben, and I started from nothing and created the successful Fortune Cosmetics empire.

But fame and wealth aren't everything—family comes first. My children and grandchildren's happiness is most important to me. And I'll do anything—even a little meddling—to make sure they always land on their feet.

Nothing—and no one—will stand in the way of whatever I set out to do....

A LETTER FROM THE AUTHOR

Dear Reader,

I am so proud and pleased to have been asked to write the launch title for Fortune's Children. I think this is a fast, entertaining, sexy, exciting series—and I certainly had a lot of fun doing *Hired Husband*. I hope you enjoy it!

It's been said many times that the rich are different. Yet when I sat down to write about Caroline Fortune, I didn't find that to be true at all. She brought the same hopes and fears to her relationship with Nick Valkov that I think all of us do in our own lives.

It was Nick who surprised me. When I was told by Silhouette that my hero was a chemist, I had the same mental image Caroline thought Nick *should* conjure up: dull, boring, puttering away in some dusty old laboratory piled high with books and beakers. So much for stereotypes. I don't think I'll ever look at a chemist in quite the same way again!

Caroline and Nick's marriage starts out as one of convenience and grows to be a love match because they have the chance to become friends. If Fortune's Children has a message, I believe it's that husbands aren't just husbands, and family isn't just family—they are, or should be, our friends, as well. I think that sometimes in the hustle and bustle of our everyday lives, we tend to forget that. Caroline and Nick remember. May you all be just as fortunate in your own lives!

Rebecca Brandewine

Rebecca Brandewyne
HIRED HUSBAND

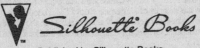

Published by Silhouette Books

America's Publisher of Contemporary Romance

For my stepfather,
Verne.
With love.

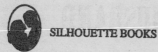

SILHOUETTE BOOKS

HIRED HUSBAND

Copyright © 1996 by Harlequin Books S.A.

ISBN 0-373-50177-3

Special thanks and acknowledgment to Rebecca Brandewyne
for her contribution to the Fortune's Children series.

Removable book marker strip is covered under U.S. Reissue
Patent No. 34,759.

REBECCA BRANDEWYNE

New York Times bestselling author Rebecca Brandewyne began her first romance novel at just twenty-one years of age, while finishing her Master of Arts degree in communications. Rebecca has since gone on to write eighteen books and five novellas, all of which have been bestsellers. Her versatility as an author has inspired effortless jumps between the genres of contemporary, historical and Gothic fiction, and her various works have appeared on bestseller lists for the *New York Times, Publishers Weekly,* the *Los Angeles Times* and *Magazine & Bookseller,* among many others.

Rebecca has come a long way from her roots as a self-professed country girl. She is now heralded as one of the world's leading romance authors, equally adept at easing her stories into existing history, setting them squarely in the present or creating future worlds for her characters. With more than 8.5 million copies of her books in print worldwide, Rebecca's novels have reached 60 countries around the globe.

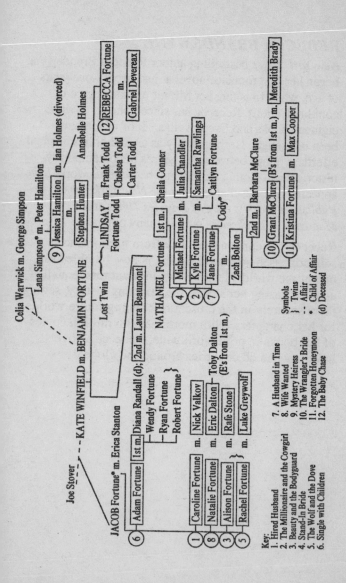

Celia Warwick m. George Simpson

Lana Simpson* m. Peter Hamilton

Joe Stover

- - KATE WINFIELD m. BENJAMIN FORTUNE

(9) Jessica Hamilton m. Ian Holmes (divorced)

Stephen Hunter

Annabelle Holmes

LINDSAY m. Frank Todd

Fortune Todd ─ Chelsea Todd
                Carter Todd

(12) REBECCA Fortune
       m.
     Gabriel Devereax

Lost Twin

NATHANIEL Fortune

(4) Michael Fortune 1st m. Sheila Conner

     Julia Chandler
     m.
(2) Kyle Fortune Samantha Rawlings

(7) Jane Fortune Caitlyn Fortune
     m.   Cody*
   Zach Bolton

(10) Grant McClure (B's from 1st m.) m. Meredith Brady

2nd m. Barbara McClure

(11) Kristina Fortune m. Max Cooper

JACOB Fortune* m. Erica Stanton

(6) Adam Fortune 1st m. Diana Randall (d); 2nd m. Laura Beaumont

Wendy Fortune
Ryan Fortune }
Robert Fortune

(1) Caroline Fortune m. Nick Valkov

(8) Natalie Fortune m. Eric Dalton ─ Toby Dalton
                                        (E's from 1st m.)

(3) Alison Fortune m. Rafe Stone

(5) Rachel Fortune m. Luke Greywolf

Symbols
} Twins
-- Affair
• Child of Affair
(d) Deceased

Key:
1. Hired Husband
2. The Millionaire and the Cowgirl
3. Beauty and the Bodyguard
4. Stand-In Bride
5. The Wolf and the Dove
6. Single with Children
7. A Husband in Time
8. Wife Wanted
9. Mystery Heiress
10. The Wrangler's Bride
11. Forgotten Honeymoon
12. The Baby Chase

FORTUNE'S Children

Meet the Fortunes—three generations of a family with a legacy of wealth, influence and power. As they unite to face an unknown enemy, shocking family secrets are revealed...and passionate new romances are ignited.

KATE FORTUNE: Fearless matriarch of the Fortune clan—until her plane crashes and the family is left to make the most of her legacy. Her children and grandchildren inherit gifts that become touchstones for happiness...and romance.

CAROLINE FORTUNE: The dynamic marketing executive for Fortune Cosmetics, she has no time for romance. But she'll do anything to save the family business, including marrying—in name only—a sexy scientist.

NICK VALKOV: Fortune's top chemist needs a bride—and Caroline needs a protector. But what starts as a green card marriage turns into so much more....

KYLE FORTUNE: Playboy millionaire. When he inherits a Wyoming ranch from his grandmother, can this city slicker roll up his sleeves and turn into a genuine cowboy?

LIZ JONES—
CELEBRITY GOSSIP

Kate Fortune, CEO of Fortune Cosmetics, was on her way to clinch what close friends have hinted is a major business coup when her private plane suddenly crashed. The family isn't saying anything, but rumor has it that Kate's missing...and could be dead!

The fabulously wealthy Fortune family has come face-to-face with plenty of turmoil in recent days...and some are saying that this crash was no accident. Just last week a top Fortune Cosmetics employee was faced with deportation. Next, a very mysterious fire exploded in the company lab.

Is someone out to ruin the Fortune family? And how will they survive the secrets and scandal that threaten their reputations? And with Kate's crash, *I* hear some Fortune family members are worried about their lives.

Prologue

"Now, Duckie," the low voice on the telephone purred throatily. "I know that with all your connections, you must have a friend or two at the INS. And really, what I'm asking is only a teeny, tiny favor, one that involves no risk at all to you or to anybody at the INS, either, for that matter. After all, who could possibly care whether one lone Russian male has his green card revoked? You can say you got a tip from an anonymous informer, which led you to believe that Dr. Nicolai Valkov is a former KGB agent or is hooked up with the Russian mob in this country or something. Whatever. Just as long as he's viewed as an undesirable alien and deported. The INS won't question your word, Duckie...the word of one of the most powerful senators on Capitol Hill. So I know you can do it...that you can get rid of Nick Valkov for me. And of course, it goes without saying that I'd be ever so...grateful to you. So grateful, in fact, that I'd have to make a special trip out to Washington just to see you, Duckie. We'll have our own private celebration, just the two of us. I'll bring champagne—and that lit-tle black boudoir ensemble of mine you like so much...."

As he leaned back in the big burgundy-leather chair before his massive, antique oak desk, Senator Don-ald Devane closed his eyes at the images evoked by the husky voice on the other end of the telephone. His breath was harsh and labored. His heart hammered with excitement, and his groin tightened unbearably as he remembered their last "celebration"—and the black outfit. His palm sweated profusely on the re-ceiver as he made a long attempt to clear his throat, choked with anticipation and arousal. At last, he managed to speak.

"I...ah...do, in fact, have a friend or two at the INS. So I don't see why I couldn't make those ar-rangements for you. A casual word dropped here or there. No, that shouldn't pose any problem whatso-ever. Consider Nick Valkov as good as on a plane back to Russia at this very moment."

"Oh, Duckie, I knew my faith in you wasn't mis-placed. Call me just as soon as you've got everything fixed up with the INS, and *I'll* be on the next plane out to Washington, I promise. Until then, keep my side of the bed warm and have sweet dreams about me...as I will about you. See you soon, Duckie." A soft, se-ductive laugh echoed from the receiver before the line went dead, leaving the dial tone buzzing in the sena-tor's ear.

After he had got his breathing and heartbeat back under control, Donald Devane punched one of the intercom buttons on his telephone, directing his secretary to put through a call for him to the Immigration and Naturalization Service bureau.

Some minutes later, a computer at the INS began the process that would revoke the green card of one Dr. Nicolai Valkov, currently director of research and development at Fortune Cosmetics—and therefore, unbeknown to him, a spoke in somebody's wheel.

One

Minneapolis, Minnesota

As Caroline Fortune wheeled her sedate dark blue Volvo into the underground parking lot of the towering, glass-and-steel structure that housed the global headquarters of Fortune Cosmetics, she glanced anxiously at her gold Piaget wristwatch. An accident on the snowy freeway had caused rush-hour traffic to be a nightmare this morning. As a result, she could be late for her 9:00 a.m. meeting—and if there were one thing her grandmother, Kate Winfield Fortune, simply couldn't abide, it was slack, unprofessional behavior on the job.

And lateness was the sign of a sloppy, disorganized schedule.

Involuntarily, Caroline shuddered at the thought of her grandmother's infamous wrath being unleashed upon her. The stern rebuke would be precise, apropos and scathing, she knew, delivered with coolly raised, condemnatory eyebrows and in icy tones of haughty grandeur that had in the past reduced many an executive—even male ones—at Fortune Cosmetics not only to obsequious apologies, but even to tears. Caroline had seen it happen on more than one occasion, although, much to her gratitude and relief, she herself was seldom a target of her grandmother's anger.

And she wouldn't be this morning, either, not if she could help it. That would be a disastrous way to start out the new year.

Grabbing her Louis Vuitton tote bag and her black leather portfolio from the front passenger seat, Caroline slipped gracefully from the Volvo and slammed the door. The heels of her Maud Frizon pumps clicked briskly on the concrete floor as she hurried toward the bank of elevators that would take her up into the skyscraper owned by her family. She pressed the Up button on the wall, muttering under her breath as several minutes seemed to tick by before, at last, a chime sounded and a pair of elevator doors slid open to admit her.

Presently, she was rushing down the long, plushly carpeted corridors of one of the hushed upper floors, toward the conference room where the meeting was scheduled.

By now, Caroline had her portfolio open and was leafing through it as she hastened along, reviewing the notes she had prepared for her presentation. So she didn't see Dr. Nicolai Valkov until she literally ran right into him. Like her, he had his head bent over his own portfolio, not watching where he was going, either; as the two of them collided, both their portfolios and the papers inside went flying.

At the unexpected impact, Caroline lost her balance, stumbled, and would have fallen had not Nick's strong, sure hands abruptly shot out, grabbing hold of her and pulling her close to steady her. She gasped, startled and stricken, as she came up hard against his broad chest, lean hips and corded thighs, her face just inches from his own—as though they were lovers about to kiss.

Caroline had never been so close to Nick Valkov before, and in that instant, she was acutely aware of him—not just as a fellow employee of Fortune Cosmetics, but also as a man. Of how tall and ruggedly handsome he was, dressed in an elegant, pin-striped black suit cut in the European fashion, a crisp white shirt, a foulard tie and a pair of Cole Haan loafers. Of how dark his thick, glossy hair and his deep-set eyes framed by raven-wing brows were—so dark that they were almost black, despite the bright fluorescent lights that blazed overhead. Of the whiteness of his straight teeth against his bronzed skin as a brazen, mocking grin slowly curved his wide, sensual mouth.

"Actually, I *was* hoping for a sweet roll this morning—but I daresay you would prove even tastier, Ms. Fortune," Nick drawled impertinently, his low, silky voice tinged with a faint accent born of the fact that Russian, not English, was his native language.

At his words, Caroline flushed painfully, embarrassed and annoyed. If there was one person she always attempted to avoid at Fortune Cosmetics, it was Nick Valkov.

Following the breakup of the Soviet Union, he had emigrated to the United States, where her grandmother had hired him to direct the company's research and development department. Since that time, Nick had constantly demonstrated marked, traditional Old World tendencies that had led Caroline to believe he not only had no use for equal rights, but also would actually have been more than happy to turn back the clock several centuries where females were concerned. She thought his remark was typical of his attitude toward women: insolent, arrogant and domineering. Really, the man was simply insufferable!

Caroline couldn't imagine what had prompted her grandmother to hire him—and at a highly generous salary—except that Nick Valkov was considered one of the foremost chemists anywhere on the planet. Deep inside, Caroline knew that no matter how he behaved, Fortune Cosmetics was really extremely lucky to have him. Still, that didn't give him the right to manhandle and insult her!

"I assure you that you would find me more bitter than a cup of the strongest black coffee, Dr. Valkov," she insisted now, attempting without success to free her trembling body from his steely grip, which continued to hold her so near that she could feel his heart beating steadily in his chest—and knew he must be equally able to feel the erratic hammering of her own.

"Oh, I'm willing to wager there's more sugar and cream to you than you let on, Ms. Fortune." To her utter mortification and outrage, she felt one of Nick's hands slide insidiously up her back and nape, to her luxuriant mass of sable hair, done up in a stylish French twist. "You know so much about fashion," he murmured, eyeing her assessingly and pointedly ignoring her indignation and efforts to escape from him. "So why do you always wear your hair like this . . . so tightly wrapped and severe? I've never seen it down. That's the way it needs to be worn, you know . . . soft, loose, tangled around your face. As it is, your hair fairly cries out for a man to take the pins from it, so he can see how long it is. Does it fall past your shoulders?" He quirked one eyebrow inquisitively, a mocking half smile still twisting his lips, letting her know he was enjoying her obvious discomfiture. "You aren't going to tell me, are you. What a pity. Because my guess is that it does—and I'd like to know if I'm right. And these glasses." He indicated the large, square tortoiseshell frames perched on her slender, classic nose. "I think you use them to hide behind more than you do to see. I'll bet you don't actually even need them at all."

Caroline felt the blush that had yet to leave her cheeks deepen betrayingly, its heat seeming to spread throughout her entire body. Damn the man! Why must he be so infuriatingly audacious and perceptive? Because what Nick suspected was true: her hair *did* fall below her shoulders, and the prescription in her lenses *was* so light as to be negligible. She customarily wore both the French twist and the glasses solely because she felt they gave her a more businesslike appearance, a no-nonsense image she had determinedly cultivated to conceal her vulnerable, romantic inner self from the rest of the world—from men in particular.

"Dr. Valkov," Caroline said frostily, forcing herself to marshal her wits and composure, "not only am I *not* even remotely interested in what you think, but neither of us has time to stand here exchanging idle chitchat—that is, unless you care to be the recipient of one of my grandmother's notorious dressing-downs. I, however, do not. Therefore, I would appreciate it if you would release me, so that I, at least, can make our nine o'clock meeting on time. There are currently less than five minutes to spare."

"The meeting." Nick started slightly at the reminder. "Would you believe that bumping into you drove it completely from my mind, Ms. Fortune?" He let her go then, kneeling to help her retrieve and sort out all the papers that had scattered from the two portfolios.

Once she and he finally had everything straightened out, they entered the conference room together, where Caroline was dismayed to observe that she and

Nick were the very last ones to arrive. Her grandmother sat at the head of the huge, Honduras-
mahogany conference table. She was flanked by Caroline's father, Jacob Fortune, who was Kate's eldest
son and the president of Fortune Cosmetics, and
Sterling Foster, who was Kate's attorney and closest
friend. Sprawled in a chair to one side and looking as
though he were nursing a pounding hangover was
Caroline's playboy cousin Kyle, his suit jacket already discarded and his collar and tie loosened, despite the early hour.

Although seventy, Kate Winfield Fortune was anything but old and decrepit. She had a striking, barely
wrinkled face born of both excellent bone structure
and the best cosmetics and skin care money could buy.
As usual, her rich, wine red hair, lightly streaked with
gray, was upswept in a classic Gibson girl that accen-
tuated the high cheekbones and flawless, creamy skin
Caroline herself had inherited.

Despite that Kate was slim and small in stature, her
feisty, dynamic personality ensured that she dominated her surroundings. Her sparkling, shrewd blue
eyes were evidence to the fact that her vivacity and
energy were those of a woman half her age and that
her mind was still as sharp as the proverbial tack. Nobody put anything past Kate Winfield Fortune.

She was the CEO of the entire Fortune holdings,
which included not only Fortune Cosmetics, an en-
terprise she herself had founded years ago, but also a

worldwide construction and development corpora-
tion, and interests in oil and ranching. More than
anyone else in the extended Fortune family, Caroline
adored her grandmother. She wanted to be just like
her.

But in her heart, Caroline knew that, unfortunately, she lacked her grandmother's natural warmth,
wittiness and high spirits, her zest for life and her quest
for adventure. If Caroline had ever possessed those
attributes, they had been crushed out of her some
years back by her disastrous engagement.

She had been so young and so in love with Paul
Andersen, a colleague at Fortune Cosmetics. It had
nearly destroyed her when, by a cruel trick of fate, she
had inadvertently learned it wasn't her Paul had truly
loved, but her share of the Fortune riches.

Since that time, deeply wounded and embittered,
Caroline had resolutely steered clear of men, concen-
trating instead on her career, emulating her grandmother's business acumen, ambition and flair for
fashion. Through intelligence, savvy, hard work,
dedication and sheer determination, Caroline had
risen through the ranks to become Fortune Cosmetics' vice president of marketing.

And she knew she was good at her job, that she had
earned her position. Because her grandmother didn't
believe in handing anybody—not even family—anything on a silver platter.

"Good morning, everyone." Caroline quickly drew off her expensive leather gloves and elegant camel wool coat, laying them aside, trying to still the wild thudding of her heart, the agitated quivering of her body, as Nick's dark glance raked her again appraisingly. "I hope you haven't been waiting too long. The snow caused an accident on the freeway this morning, tying up traffic forever, or I would have been here sooner."

"Not to mention the fact that Ms. Fortune and I had a small collision of our own out in the hall." Nick's mouth turned down wryly at the corners as he surveyed Caroline, and he shook his head at her imperceptibly, so she knew he disapproved not only of her hair and glasses, but also of her classically tailored Chanel suit and cream-colored silk blouse.

She had the horrible, unsettling impression that he was mentally stripping her naked, that he knew exactly what she looked like naked; to conceal the flush she felt creeping up once more to stain her cheeks crimson, she swiftly bent over her portfolio, which she had spread open on the conference table. She was abruptly beset by such an awful urge to box Nick's ears, to slap the smirk clean off his handsome face, that she could scarcely contain herself.

What on earth was the matter with her this morning? She was usually cool, composed and competent. It was most unlike her to be so flustered and irritated—especially by a man. The terrible traffic snarl must have rattled her more than she had suspected. She had better get hold of herself in a hurry, she told herself, or her marketing presentation was definitely going to suffer—particularly as Kyle now appeared to have fallen asleep in his chair.

At the sight of him, Caroline silently cursed the kindly impulse that had caused her some months ago to promote him to the position of her assistant. Despite that he was one of her favorite cousins, he was just like every other man she had ever known—utterly worthless and no good, she now thought hotly.

"Well, despite all the mishaps, we're still on schedule. So, since we're all assembled, shall we get started?" Kate asked briskly. "Kyle. *Kyle!* Do you care to wake up and join us this morning?" Frowning, she stared at her errant grandson censoriously as he was nudged to awareness by a surreptitious punch in the ribs, delivered by Sterling Foster. "Somehow, Kyle, I just don't think you're cut out for Fortune Cosmetics," Kate observed dryly, once he had started awake. "It's my belief that you need to be someplace where you're forced to get up at the crack of dawn, breathe great lungfuls of fresh air and work so hard all day that you're too tired for any nightlife at all—much less the wild one that seems to be affecting you for the worse these days."

"Good heavens, Grandmother. I can't think of anything less appealing than sunrises and crisp air." Yawning and rising, Kyle strolled leisurely over to the credenza along one wall, where he poured himself a cup of black coffee from the automatic coffeemaker that sat next to a Baccarat crystal pitcher of freshly squeezed orange juice and a sterling-silver tray sporting an assortment of fruits and breads. "Besides, I worked late last night."

At her grandson's words, Kate snorted her disbelief but, mercifully, chose not to pursue the subject. Instead, she directed peremptorily, "Nick, you begin, why don't you. How is my secret youth formula progressing?"

"Very well, actually." Confidently, Nick stood, moving around the conference table to the computerized video-presentation equipment, into whose drive he inserted a diskette. After a few moments, the huge monitor on the stand was filled with a complex diagram and chemical equations Caroline could not begin to understand. Using a laser pointer, Nick explained. "You're all aware from previous meetings of the steps we've taken to date. This morning, I'm happy to report that after years of research and development, the secret youth formula is finally nearing completion. This is the formula's matrix. When combined with various properties present in the epidermis, this is what happens, according to both theory and our tests."

A click of the mouse put the big screen into motion. What followed was a thirty-minute video, detailing in layman's terms the effect of the secret youth formula upon the skin. The intricate demo ended with the reassembling of the original matrix.

"Now," Nick continued, "you will notice that the matrix is not wholly formed. The break you see here in this molecular chain—" he shone the laser pointer on the monitor "—is what I call Ingredient X, meaning that we're certain we need one last element to finish the formula. We just don't know yet what that element is, although we've managed within the past several months to narrow the range of possibilities considerably. My guess is that it won't be long at all now until we *do* isolate and identify Ingredient X, at which point the formula will be ready for market. Are there any questions?"

"So what you're saying," said Jacob Fortune, known to everyone as Jake, "is that the secret youth formula utilizes properties similar to those found in Retin-A and salicylic acid, as well as alpha hydroxies like glycolic acid? But that Fortune Cosmetics' formula will go beyond those products—that it will, in fact, revolutionize the entire cosmetic market in that it will be similar, basically, to a chemical peel for which consumers previously would have needed to visit a plastic surgeon or dermatologist? And the difference is that they will now be able to perform the task themselves—both safely and relatively inexpensively—in the privacy of their own homes? Further, that the effects of Fortune Cosmetics' formula will be cumulative, that is, the longer the formula is used, the greater the benefits will prove?''

"Exactly." Nick nodded, his dark eyes gleaming with excitement. "With proper, regular use, Fortune Cosmetics' formula will, within just a matter of months, restore even the most deteriorated skin to the texture, elasticity, et cetera, that it exhibited in its late teenage to early twenties years—minus the acne, of course." The observation brought a round of appreciative chuckles. "In addition, once that youthful stage has been reached by the consumer, consistent use of the product a few times a week will maintain the skin at that level—which means, of course, that the majority of consumers will be steady customers.

"Because the formula is, in essence, a chemical peel, it will require FDA approval. However, all our tests have led us to believe that won't be a problem. As you know, we've worked closely with the FDA all along, both to ensure conformity with all their rules and regulations, and to keep them apprised of our test results. Sterling can fill you in on all those legalities. In addition, we'll undoubtedly have several patents granted—which will tend to slow down our competition for quite a while. I expect our market share to increase substantially as a result." Nick grinned wickedly, bringing a scowl to Caroline's face as she watched him.

It just wasn't right for any man to be so damned attractive, she thought—especially when that handsomeness was coupled with an imperious attitude and undeniable intelligence. The man was brilliant; she had to give him credit for that.

Opening his portfolio, Nick withdrew several identical bound reports, which he passed around the conference table, announcing, "I have, of course, prepared full written summaries of my presentation for you all."

"Excellent." Kate beamed her approval. "You've done an outstanding job, Nick! I have every confidence that you will shortly discover the missing Ingredient X. Further, I know I speak for all of us here at Fortune Cosmetics when I say how much I deeply appreciate your dedication to the job and all the contributions you've made to the company since coming aboard. Keep up the good work! And keep me informed of your progress, won't you? Now, speaking of our market share...Caroline, is your advertising campaign ready for the launch of our secret youth formula?"

"Yes, Grandmother, it is." Smoothing her skirt, Caroline rose to make her way to the computerized video-presentation equipment while Nick pressed the button on the drive to release his diskette, which he slipped into his portfolio.

Then he strolled over to the credenza. "Ah...sweet rolls!" he exclaimed, glancing rakishly beneath hooded lids at Caroline.

Much to her irritation and discomposure, she felt herself blush as furiously again as she had earlier outside in the corridor, and her fingers were suddenly so clumsy that she dropped upon the floor the diskette she was attempting to insert. When she bent to retrieve the diskette, she accidentally knocked her portfolio from the conference table, too, sending all her papers flying once more.

Swearing under her breath, she shot Nick the proverbial look that could have killed, causing him to grin hugely.

"Here, let me help you, Ms. Fortune." He knelt beside her to gather up the fallen papers. Between his teeth, he now gripped one of the sweet rolls from the sterling-silver tray on the credenza.

It was all Caroline could do to prevent herself from shoving the sweet roll down his throat. She was embarrassedly aware of her grandmother, father, cousin and Sterling watching her and Nick curiously, clearly wondering what, if anything, might be between the two of them.

While Fortune Cosmetics did not have a company policy against employee fraternization, Caroline could not help but remember what had happened with Paul Andersen and how disappointed her grandmother and father both had been in her judgment. Her mistake with Paul had caused them to look over her shoulder for months afterward, double-checking the decisions she had made on the job.

Were they even now sitting there knowing—as they had known about Paul and she had not—that Nick Valkov was a fortune hunter, too, or otherwise unsuitable in some fashion? Were they even now questioning her judgment again?

That thought incensed Caroline, reminding her why she had always gone out of her way to avoid Nick—and every other man at Fortune Cosmetics.

Beneath the edge of the conference table, she glowered darkly at Nick. In response, he broke off a piece of the sweet roll, offering it to her, while he ate his own portion with relish, deliberately savoring it. Despite herself, she felt her eyes drawn to his sulky, sensuous mouth, his tongue that licked the sticky icing from his long, elegant fingers. Unbidden, a sudden image of him doing wild, sexy things to her with those lips and tongue rose in her mind, mortifying her and setting the pulse at the hollow of her throat to fluttering wildly.

Shaking her head curtly at the proffered sweet roll, she bent over her scattered papers, feeling the heat of her blush deepen and spread, stricken by the terrible, unnerving suspicion that Nick had somehow seen the mental picture she had had of the two of them together.

From beneath her long, thick sooty lashes, she glanced at him surreptitiously. He was no longer grinning, which should have relieved her—and would have—except that now his dark eyes glittered with speculation as he stared at her, as though he had never

really looked at her before and suddenly saw a great
deal to interest him.

"Your papers, Ms. Fortune," Nick said softly as he
handed them to her. One powerful, slender hand
reached out, took hold of her arm. Caroline was so
startled and unsettled by their physical contact that she
only barely restrained herself from jerking away from
him as he assisted her to her feet.

"Thank you, Dr. Valkov," she replied as cooly as
she could manage, silently cursing the fact that her
hand trembled as she jammed her diskette into the
drive. She cleared her throat nervously. Then, determinedly ignoring Nick, she began her presentation.
"As you're all aware, we've had several names for the
secret youth formula under consideration. Based on
the marketing campaign that I and my department
have developed, however, this is the name we suggest
that you approve."

A click of the mouse brought her own presentation
to the monitor, and superimposed over the Fortune
Cosmetics' logo, the words *Fabulous Face* flashed on
the screen.

After a moment, the video itself unfolded, explaining the concept for the marketing campaign, then fo-
cusing on the actual print and television advertising.
The proposed TV commercial started with a closeup
of Caroline's sister Allison—who was Fortune Cosmetics' top supermodel—and a low, seductively con-
fiding voice-over that asked, "What's her secret?"

Then the spiel describing the new product ensued as several different women of various nationalities and ages, all the models beautiful and youthful-looking, were shown in a number of settings, both at work and play. More than one of the women had a tall, handsome man at her side. Tucked discreetly into each scene was a shot of the product itself, packaged in an appealing, gilded, heavy glass container designed in Fortune Cosmetics' signature style.

Sixty seconds later, the proposed commercial ended with the voice-over announcing, "And now that you know her secret, you, too, can be one of Fortune's Fabulous Faces."

Much to Caroline's pleasure, at the video's completion, the room erupted in applause.

"It's wonderful!" Kate crowed, laughing like a gleeful child. "Precisely what we want to get across to the consumer... that any woman who uses our secret youth formula can have a fabulous face! That's it! That's exactly what we'll call it—Fabulous Face! Sterling, make a note to register that name right away. Oh, it's a clever television commercial, Caroline, beautiful, sensuous, a little mysterious, not clinical at all, even though you manage to get the primary points of the product across.... And the magazine layouts you've designed are gorgeous and glamorous yet down-to-earth at the same time, so they won't make the average woman feel that a fabulous face is beyond her reach. I am just absolutely delighted—and so proud of you, Caroline! Excellent work! Keep it up!''

Even more than her grandmother's praise, Caroline was thrilled to hear her father's compliments when he chimed in exuberantly. Jake was very much aware of his position in both the family and Fortune Cosmetics. He had, she knew, given up his own dreams to take charge of the company, resolutely dedicating himself over the years to making it a tremendous success. As a result, he had demanding, frequently impossible expectations, and Caroline understood that she had always taken second place in his heart, that it was her older brother, Adam, whom Jake would have preferred to have seen at Fortune Cosmetics, being groomed as its heir.

But Adam had always been at odds with their father and had never wanted anything to do with any of the family businesses. At eighteen, her brother had rebelled and struck out on his own, joining the military. That had been a bitter disappointment to Jake. And although ever since then, Caroline had striven almost desperately to make up for Adam's desertion, to win her father's approval, today was the first time she felt she had truly succeeded. More than anyone else at the company, she thought, Jake realized just how much was riding on the secret youth formula that would prove the culmination of all Kate had ever hoped to achieve in life.

After a few more minutes of discussion, the meeting adjourned, everybody agreeing that the new product was wonderfully on track and extremely close now to becoming a reality.

"Before you all leave, I want to remind you that positively everything connected with the secret youth formula is to remain strictly confidential," Kate insisted as she gathered up her copies of Nick's and Caroline's presentation reports. "We all know the hazards of industrial espionage, and I don't want any of our competitors getting wind of Fabulous Face until it hits the market. We're going to blow them away with this one! I can feel it in my bones. Oh, how I'd love to see our competitors' expressions when they find out about Fabulous Face! They're just absolutely going to croak!" Kate giggled again like a mischievous child at the notion.

Then she swept from the conference room, Sterling trailing along in her wake, Jake following behind.

"Kyle, I need to see you in my office for a few minutes," Caroline announced hastily, not wanting to be left alone with Nick Valkov. Even so, her heart sank as she thought of what she must say to her wayward cousin. Over the years, she had become very adept at reading between the lines of her grandmother's words. So, sadly, Caroline had recognized that Kate's seemingly innocent observations about Kyle earlier had, in reality, been her grandmother's subtle way of instructing her to fire her cousin.

In her heart, Caroline knew that what Kate had said was true: Kyle just didn't fit in at Fortune Cosmetics, wasn't cut out for the cutthroat corporate world. Not only did he play around a great deal more than he worked, but he had also had a string of affairs and one-night stands with more than one of the supermodels signed to exclusive, multimillion-dollar contracts with the company.

Recently, Danielle Duvalier—who rivaled even Caroline's sister Allison for face and name recognition in the marketplace—had been so devastated by her breakup with Kyle that she had nearly suffered a nervous breakdown, and Caroline had been forced to send her to the Bahamas to recuperate.

Kyle's falling asleep at this morning's meeting was simply the last straw.

So, no matter how callous and cruel it seemed to Caroline, she realized she had to get rid of her cousin. Now, as she and Kyle entered her office together, she mentally steeled herself for the unpleasant task. She loathed firing anybody.

"Close the door and sit down, Kyle," she directed as she hung her coat in the closet of her luxurious corner office with its wide windows overlooking the Twin Cities and the Mississippi River, which separated Minneapolis and St. Paul at its confluence with the Minnesota River. As Kyle cast his suit jacket aside and sat down in one of the two plush chairs before her elegant, cherry-wood Queen Anne desk, Caroline took her own seat behind it, drawing a deep breath before she spoke again. "Kyle, you know you're one of my favorite cousins," she began, only to have him interrupt with a wry grin.

"But I'm not living up to your expectations, am I? I've let you down in more ways than one, especially by falling asleep at the conference table earlier, and now you've got to fire me. Oh, don't look so surprised and chagrined, Caro. You're not the only one who's got a handle on Grandmother and what she meant this morning with her observations about my character. And to tell you the truth, I've sensed this day was coming. In a way, I'm actually even glad and relieved that it's here. It's saved me from quitting." Kyle paused for a moment, running his hand through his sun-streaked hair, his smile rueful but his blue eyes sober.

"I know you gave me a chance, Caro, and for your sake, I'm sorry your promoting me to your assistant hasn't worked out. But unfortunately, Grandmother was right. I just don't belong here at Fortune Cosmetics. Hell. I'm starting to believe I don't belong *anywhere!* Frankly, the fascination of my jet-setting nightlife began to pall some time ago. But I just can't seem to find anything more worthwhile to replace it. If you want to know the truth, I'm restless and bored to tears. Honestly, half the time, I feel like just chucking it all and going off to hole up in the wild somewhere, becoming a mountain man or something."

"Well, why don't you, then?" Caroline asked, her brow knitted with caring and concern. "Just because you have money doesn't mean you have to be a playboy all your life, Kyle."

"I know that. But you know how we Fortunes are, Caro. From Grandmother on down, we're all a spoiled, stubborn lot, each of us in our own fashion determined to have our own way, no matter how foolish. Look at Adam, running off to join the army. Look at you, hiding behind those glasses you don't need and cutting yourself off from men all because of that worthless Paul Andersen. Oh, don't get me wrong. I'm not criticizing you, Caro. I'm commiserating. God knows, I haven't done any better myself in the love department," Kyle stated glumly. "I need to get out less, and you need to get out more—and that's a fact. I noticed Nick Valkov seemed quite taken with you this morning."

At his words, Caroline felt a blush once more creeping up to stain her cheeks. She frowned at her cousin censoriously. "That's ridiculous! Why, the man's as big a playboy as you, Kyle. He could have any woman he wanted. Why should he be interested in me?"

"Well, if you'd ever take off those stupid glasses, let down your hair and look in the mirror once in a while, Caro, you'd know. You're as beautiful as Allie, damn it! You could be one of Fortune's Fabulous Faces yourself."

"Oh, Kyle, that's so sweet of you to say so. But you know it's not true."

"The hell it isn't. Why, if you weren't my cousin, I'd be tempted myself." He flashed her the devastating grin that had charmed and then broken so many hearts. "There's always something about an ice queen that makes a man want to melt her. Trust me. Nick Valkov isn't any exception. I know the signs. He's interested in taking up the challenge, all right." Kyle stood, tossing his jacket carelessly over his shoulder and jamming one hand into his trouser pocket. Then he leaned across her desk to kiss her lightly on the cheek. "So why don't you loosen up, Caro? Give the man a chance. And don't feel bad about firing me. You've done me a favor. Take care of yourself—and I'll see you around." Whistling cheerfully, he sauntered from her office, leaving her staring after him, dwelling on his words.

After a long moment, Caroline shook her head, resolutely forcing herself from her reverie. Kyle was crazy. Nick Valkov had deliberately taunted her this morning only to amuse himself at her expense. He had no real interest whatsoever in her.

Absolutely none.

Two

It was after dark when Nick Valkov pulled into the driveway of his large, elegant house situated on one of the beautiful lakes beyond Minneapolis's city limits. Pressing the button of the remote control to open one of the three doors, he parked his Mercedes-Benz in the garage. Then he went inside, taking his attaché with him. It contained paperwork from the office, along with his mail, which he had retrieved a few moments ago from his mailbox.

In the great room, whose floor-to-ceiling windows provided a panoramic view of the lake beyond, Nick stripped off his heavy wool topcoat, leather gloves, suit jacket and tie, carelessly tossing them over a chair. Then he loosened his collar and poured himself a shot of Stolichnaya vodka from the Waterford crystal decanter on the bar. Sipping the drink, he settled into one of the comfortable overstuffed chairs and flipped open his briefcase. Withdrawing his mail, he began to sort through it, pitching to one side what was obviously junk and placing the rest into a pile.

It was when he came to an envelope bearing the return address of the Immigration and Naturalization

Service that he paused, tearing it open to read the tersely worded letter inside. He was so stunned by its contents that at first he couldn't believe his eyes. He swore softly, stricken.

"No, this just can't be right! There must be some mistake somewhere!" he insisted to himself. Both anger and fear roiled inside him as he mentally watched all his hopes, dreams and plans for the future going up in smoke, vanishing as though they had never been.

He had been declared an undesirable alien and was going to be deported from the United States! Sent back to Russia! He was to surrender himself to the nearest INS office, bringing his passport and green card with him. These instructions were followed by stern warnings of the legal measures that would be taken against him if he disobeyed.

Nick was devastated. Although the letter did not precisely come right out and say so, it hinted that he had been identified as a former KGB agent—which wasn't true in the least. The very idea was ridiculous! He was a chemist—and a damned good one—not a spy! Still, if he were to remain in the United States, he had no doubt that he was, at the very least, facing a protracted, expensive legal battle to prove himself innocent of whatever accusations had been made against him.

The notion of returning to his own country held no appeal whatsoever. Ever since the breakup of the Soviet Union, Russia had been in a state of political turmoil. Nick did miss his homeland—which was why Minnesota, with all its wintry frozen lakes and snowy countryside—had drawn him to settle in the Twin Cities area. But he did *not* in the least long for the constant upheaval born of the ideological struggles of Russia's government officials.

Reaching for the telephone, Nick picked up the receiver and punched in the number of Kate Fortune's private line at the office. He let the telephone ring endlessly, but there was no response, so he finally tried her at home. When she answered, he spoke, relieved to have caught her.

"Kate? It's Nick Valkov. I'm sorry to disturb you at home, but something important has come up, which I thought you would want to know about right away. Is this a good time to talk—or do you have plans for the evening?"

"Actually, Sterling and I were just about to have a quiet dinner here at home, but if necessary, I can have the housekeeper set it back for a while.

"Hold on a minute, Nick," she continued briskly, "while I let Sterling know, so he can give instructions to Mrs. Brant." She placed her hand over the receiver to muffle the sound of her calling out to Sterling. Then she spoke to Nick again. "Now, why don't you tell me what's up?"

He explained about the letter from the INS, finishing with, "Needless to say, I'm very upset about all this, Kate—not to mention just utterly baffled. I simply can't imagine where the INS might have got the idea that I was a former KGB agent, for heaven's sake! Of course, I did do chemical research and development for the government—but it was never anything of a sensitive nature. I was then and still am staunchly against chemical warfare, and I have never assisted nor would I ever assist any government in developing anything of that sort. Even so, I suppose it's possible somebody's got the mistaken notion that I aided and abetted my homeland in that capacity and somehow confused my work with some secretive KGB operation.

"At any rate, because of my involvement with Fabulous Face and its importance to you, I thought I'd better let you know about all this immediately, Kate." Nick sighed heavily as, reaching for his discarded suit jacket, he withdrew a pack of Player's cigarettes from the inside pocket. Shaking one out, he lit up, inhaling deeply, then blowing a cloud of smoke into the air.

"I thought you were going to quit smoking," Kate scolded like a mother hen as she heard the sound of his exhaled breath.

"Well, I was. I mean ... I am. But damn it, Kate! This news from the INS has put me under a real strain. I don't want to go back to Russia—and I certainly don't want to lose my position at Fortune Cosmetics because I'm so involved in a legal battle that I can't do my job!"

"You don't need to worry about that, Nick. We're so close now to completing my secret youth formula that you can be assured I don't intend to let you escape from Fortune Cosmetics. We'll just have to find some way of circumventing the INS, that's all.

"Sterling!" Kate called, one hand muffling the receiver again. "Pick up the extension, so you can get in on this discussion. The INS thinks Nick's a former KGB agent, and they're attempting to deport him— and I'm not going to lose my foremost chemist. Not only is he too valuable to the company, but I just can't let him get away with all that knowledge he's got in his head about Fabulous Face," Kate declared, chuckling, removing her hand from the receiver. "Some foreign government might grab him and steal my secret youth formula, turn it into an aging cream instead. Then women everywhere would find their skin wrinkling up rather than smoothing out—and that *would* start World War Three!"

Despite himself, Nick couldn't help but laugh. "That's right, Kate," he agreed. "It's all a fiendish master plot. That's why I don't have a wife or even a steady girlfriend. I plan to be one of the lucky men who survives, who isn't done in by a thoroughly enraged woman."

"But of course, that's precisely what you need, Nick." Sterling spoke from the extension he had picked up to join in the conversation. "Not an enraged woman, but a wife, I mean. That would be the solution to all your problems."

"A *wife?*" Nick exclaimed, dismayed. "Now, why would I want one of those, Sterling?"

"Because even if you *were* a former KGB agent, if you were married to an American citizen, the INS couldn't do anything to you. You'd be in this country legally, and you wouldn't need a green card, so they couldn't deport you. That's the law," the attorney elucidated.

"So... what? I'm supposed to just pick some woman off the street and ask her to marry me?" Nick gibed. "Sterling, you surely can't imagine that the INS is going to believe that upon receipt of their letter, I just suddenly fell in love and found a wife. They'll know it's a setup."

"I agree," Kate said, the wheels of her sharp mind churning furiously. "That's why we'll need to go about this very carefully and keep it as quiet as possible—keep it all in the family, so to speak."

"Kate, what are you thinking?" Sterling queried suspiciously. He had known her for so many years that he was well aware of how her mind worked, so even as he asked the question, he had some inkling of where she was headed.

"I'm thinking that I have several beautiful grand-daughters, many of whom are single—and that at least two of them, Caroline and Allison, work for Fortune Cosmetics, besides. Now, Allison is extremely high profile, so she isn't a good choice at all. But Caroline...Caroline has always been very publicity shy. She is, as you both know, one of the movers and shakers behind the scenes of the Fortune empire, vice president of marketing at Fortune Cosmetics—*and* intimately involved in the development of Fabulous Face. She's not married. And it didn't seem to me this morning that you were too averse to her, Nick.''

Nick didn't know what to say. He felt as though he were dreaming. But shaking his head to clear it didn't cause him suddenly to wake up in his bed. The idea that he might marry Caroline Fortune—with Kate's blessing—seemed so fantastic as to be unreal.

Today was by no means the first time he had ever noticed Caroline. But just as she had this morning, she had always rejected the tentative overtures he had made to her in the past, shutting him down cold.

In the corridors of the Fortune Cosmetics building, she was known behind her back as the Ice Queen. She represented a challenge to every man at the company. But since her disastrous affair with Paul Andersen, she had let no man get close to her.

''Nick.'' Kate's voice startled him from his reverie. ''You're not saying anything. Do you find the idea of marrying my granddaughter Caroline so objectionable, then, that you can't bring yourself to tell me, for fear of offending me?''

He cleared his throat, took another long drag from his cigarette. ''No, it's...ah...not that at all, Kate.

Among other things, Caroline is quite lovely, creative and intelligent—and most men would consider themselves lucky to have her. But...well, her past relationship with Paul Andersen is pretty common knowledge at Fortune Cosmetics, as is the fact that ever since then, she's held men at arm's length. So I just simply can't imagine that she would agree to this wild scheme of yours."

"Well, we won't know until we ask her. What's important at the moment is whether you're willing to consider it, Nick. To paraphrase your own words about Caroline, you're a handsome, creative, intelligent man—and most women would consider themselves lucky to have you. But from what I hear, you pretty much play the field. And of course, that will no longer be an option for you if you marry my granddaughter." Kate's pleasant but firm tone made it plain that she would expect Nick to treat Caroline with every respect and consideration due her as his wife, even though theirs would be a marriage of convenience rather than one born of love.

"Of course, if I agreed to marry Caroline, I would do so with every intention of settling down and doing all that's right and expected, Kate." Nick was indignant that his employer might have thought otherwise. "I just don't know if this is such a good idea, that's all. Caroline and I hardly even know each other, for pity's sake."

"Well, why don't you give it some thought, Nick. Sleep on it, and let me know your decision tomorrow morning. In the meantime, I'll have Sterling start checking into the various legalities of the matter. After all, there's no point in even considering the idea if the INS is going to be able to declare the marriage a sham and deport you, anyway. I'll also speak to Jake, let him know what's happening. The first thing I want you to do when you get into the office tomorrow morning, Nick, is to clear your calendar, so you can meet with Sterling and me, and possibly Jake and Caroline, as well."

"Fine. That sounds good. I'll plan on that, then," Nick replied—although, inwardly, he groaned, thinking that this whole thing had "harebrained scheme" stamped all over it. How could he possibly ask Caroline Fortune to marry him, just to save his life here in the United States? He remembered how frostily she had stared at him this morning, how coolly she had attempted to put him in his place. She would never say yes.

Not in a million years.

Three

Caroline simply couldn't believe the conversation taking place in her grandmother's luxurious penthouse office at Fortune Cosmetics. She thought she must be imagining the fact that she was sitting here listening to Kate calmly explaining Nick Valkov's troubles with the INS, as well as what seemed to all to be the only practical solution—all, that was, except for Caroline.

She thought with dismay that her grandmother must finally have slipped into senility, must surely have taken leave of her senses. The idea that she, Caroline Fortune, should marry Nick Valkov was absolutely ludicrous. She was astonished and mortified that her grandmother had even suggested it. That Kate's expression and tone clearly indicated that she expected her to comply with the proposed plan filled her with panic.

From beneath her long, thick black lashes, Caroline stole a surreptitious glance at Nick. Much to her surprise and relief, she saw that at least he wasn't sitting there grinning mockingly at her, as he had yesterday morning. Today, in fact, he actually looked as uncomfortable as she herself felt at this moment.

Caroline didn't know whether to empathize with him or to be indignant at the realization that he obviously wasn't too enthused at the prospect of becoming her husband. Despite the fact that she certainly did *not* want to become his wife, she was piqued by the realization that he didn't want to marry her—although, as an incentive to agree to the scheme, her father had offered to up Nick's salary handsomely, as well as to pay him a six-figure bonus on the wedding day.

The wedding day, Caroline thought a trifle bitterly. *The wedding deal* was more like it. Because that's exactly what this arrangement was: a business deal, pure and simple. Her grandmother and father were paying Nick Valkov to marry her, so he wouldn't get involved in a protracted legal battle with the INS and wind up being deported, unable to complete the secret youth formula of such vital importance to Fortune Cosmetics.

Why, it was worse, somehow, than if she had married Paul Andersen! Caroline told herself hotly. At least Paul had had *some* feelings for her, had cared about her as much as he was capable, even if it *had* been her money he had loved more than her.

"Caroline...you've barely said anything at all," Kate observed, not without a note of caring and compassion.

She knew it must be hard for her granddaughter to be placed in such a difficult, seemingly unpalatable position. Nevertheless, Kate intended to continue to apply pressure upon her to accept the proposed marriage. It had not escaped the older woman's keen notice how her granddaughter had withdrawn socially after her broken engagement with Paul Andersen, how she had, with a fierce, determined vengeance, thrown herself into her work, cutting herself off from all men.

Caroline was twenty-nine now—and not getting any younger, Kate thought wryly, both anxious and exasperated at the idea that her granddaughter was missing out on all life had to offer. It was not that the older woman wanted to meddle in the younger's business, but she felt that Caroline could use a push in the right direction—as could Nick Valkov, for that matter. He was in his prime and ought to be thinking about a wife and children.

Kate wanted everyone around her to be as happy as she was—and in her book, happiness included having a partner with whom to share all of life's ups and downs. "Caroline?" she said again, expectantly.

"Forgive me Grandmother." Caroline started nervously from her reverie. She wished she could speak to her mother, but Erika Fortune was out of town for the rest of the week. "I guess I haven't said very much because, quite frankly, I'm at a complete loss as to know what to say. I'm sorry for Nick's difficulties with the INS, of course. But I just can't believe there isn't some other solution to his problem."

"The trouble is that there really isn't, Caroline." Her father, Jake, spoke soberly. "Otherwise, I wouldn't have gone along with this marriage notion of Mother's and Sterling's, because it's as wild an idea as any I've ever heard. But surely you can see how Nick's being deported would affect Fortune Cosmetics at this point in time, Caro. We've invested both years and millions of dollars in the research and development of the secret youth formula. To lose Nick now, when we're so close to completion of the product, would be a devastating blow. And of course, we're talking about a marriage in name only. Once enough time has passed and the INS has lost interest in Nick, you and he can quietly divorce, and that will be the end of it."

Not for the first time, as she felt the red creeping into her cheeks, Caroline silently cursed the fact that she blushed so easily. Her father's words about her marriage to Nick being in name only had inadvertently conjured up images of the exact opposite in her mind. She had pictured her and Nick together, naked and making love. She hoped he couldn't see into her brain. But from the sudden, speculative gleam in his eyes, she suspected that he knew what she had thought. Worse, she suspected that he had thought it, too.

Because now, as though he had, indeed, read her mind, Nick asked, "Well, Ms. Fortune, what do you say? Are you going to be responsible for my being packed off to Russia or not? All I need is a simple answer. Will you marry me? Yes or no? And then we can all get back to work—which, since I may not have as much time remaining as I had thought to finish Fabulous Face, would seem expedient under the circumstances.''

Caroline swallowed hard, her heart racing, her palms sweating. Plainly, everyone expected her to agree to wed Nick. "Sterling, isn't there really any other way?" she inquired tentatively, unconsciously licking her dry lips to moisten them.

"No, not that I can see," the attorney replied, shaking his head sympathetically, his eyes understanding.

"Well, then, I suppose that given what's at stake, I don't have any choice but to say yes to this crazy scheme," Caroline said slowly. "I know how much the secret youth formula means to you and Dad both, Grandmother, and to Fortune Cosmetics. I certainly don't want to see all your hard work wasted. And after all, it's not as though it'll be a real marriage...I mean, not in any true sense of the word...." Her voice trailed away awkwardly.

"Thank you so much, Caroline. I knew I could count on you." Kate smiled and hugged her granddaughter warmly before turning to the others in the room. "Sterling, Jake, why don't the three of us go someplace else to discuss all the necessary arrangements?'' she suggested tactfully. ''Give Caroline and Nick some time alone together. I know they must have things they want to talk over between themselves at the moment.'' She glanced thoughtfully at the now officially engaged couple. ''We'll see the two of you later.''

Shortly afterward, Caroline and Nick were alone in the office, she fidgeting nervously with her skirt, unable to meet his eyes, unable even now to believe this was all happening, that it was actually real.

This man was going to become her husband. She thought she must be mad to have consented to such a plan. Unbidden, visions of her wedding night suddenly rose in her mind, and doubt gnawed at her. After all, what did she really know about Nick Valkov, other than that he was a brilliant chemist?

Even though Fortune Cosmetics ran extensive background checks on its executive personnel, what if the IRS were right and he truly *were* a former KGB agent? What if once he got his ring on her finger and his bonus money in his bank account, he decided not to keep his part of the bargain, decided he wanted to exercise his husbandly rights?

Caroline's imagination ran wild, wreaking havoc on her emotions and senses.

''I...ah...know this can't be easy for you, Ms. Fortune.'' Nick spoke at last, breaking the silence that lay heavily between them. ''And I want to take this opportunity to thank you so much for agreeing to help me out of my difficulties this way.''

''Caroline . . . my name is Caroline,'' she reminded him softly. ''If we're going to be married, you can't keep on calling me Ms. Fortune. Otherwise, the INS will know something is wrong, that our marriage is a sham—and then it will all be for nothing, won't it?''

''Yes, of course, you're absolutely right. Caroline it is, then. And I'm Nick.'' He paused for a moment, as though gathering his thoughts. Then he continued. ''Look, let's be perfectly honest with each other. This is not what either of us might have wished for and a very awkward situation for us both. But there *are* things we can do to make it easier.''

''Such as?''

''Well, for one, we can spend a little time getting to know each other better. We're going to be husband and wife, and although we're not lovers, I'd like to think we can at least be friends during the duration of our marriage. Second, there are some matters we'll have to attend to right away. I'd like us to be wed sometime this week, as for obvious reasons, I'm in a hurry and so can't really afford to wait around while we plan a huge wedding that will be publicized in all the newspapers and will wind up attracting the INS's notice, besides. I'm sure a quick trip to the court-house wasn't what you imagined for your wedding day, but under the circumstances, I know you'll agree it's for the best. We also need to figure out where we're going to live, whether you should move in with me or I should move in with you.''

"This has all been so sudden, so unexpected and unsettling that I—I really hadn't given any of that any thought," Caroline confessed, abruptly rising from her chair and striding to the bank of windows that overlooked the city below. She stared out of them blindly, still beset by a sense of unreality. "Of course I think we should at least try to be friends, and yes, the courthouse and this—this weekend will be...fine, I guess. I hadn't—I hadn't realized we'd be married so soon, but I suppose it's for the best to secure your position against the INS. As for—for living together, I have an apartment in the city, not far from Fortune Cosmetics. It's not large, but it *is* convenient.''

"For your sake, I think we should consider privacy as opposed to proximity. So I suggest you move into my house instead," Nick replied, standing and moving to join her at the windows. "It's got plenty of room, so we won't be on top of each other. Besides which, if the INS decides to investigate our marriage, it would probably be more believable for us to say that we retained your apartment because we both often work late hours at Fortune Cosmetics and needed someplace to stay overnight in the city on those occasions, than it would be for us to say that we kept my house as a weekend retreat.''

"All right." Caroline finally worked up courage enough to turn and face him. "Dr. Valkov...Nick, I have to apologize to you. I've been so busy thinking about myself that I've only just this moment realized this can't be any easier for you than it is for me. Yet you've tried to put me at ease, and I appreciate that. I want you to know that I'll try not to disrupt your life any more than necessary, and I hope you'll do the same for me."

"Agreed." He smiled down at her—a smile that did not quite reach his dark eyes, which, to her surprise, she saw were shadowed with concern for her. "However, in order to fool the INS, we *will* need to present a solid front and to concoct some story about our having fallen in love here on the job and eloped. Thank heavens you're such a sensible, prudent, reserved woman, Caroline. We can perhaps suggest that you didn't want the fuss of and attention attracted by a big society wedding, so that's why we chose to go the courthouse route."

Unexpectedly, she felt a sense of pique at Nick's characterization of her personality. She tried to tell herself it didn't matter what he thought about her. But somehow, that didn't help.

Sensible. Prudent. Reserved. Was that really how he saw her? Was that how *everybody* saw her? Caroline asked herself, distressed. Of course it was. She knew that behind her back, Fortune Cosmetics' employees referred to her as the Ice Queen.

Not for the first time, she thought it certainly didn't make her sound as though she were any fun, the kind of woman a man would want to be with. Before, she hadn't cared; she hadn't wanted a man in her life. But now, like it or not, she was going to be Nick's wife.

"I—I suppose I'm not at all the sort of woman to whom you're usually attracted."

"Actually, I find you very attractive, Caroline," Nick declared quietly. "I just think you're a little uptight, that's all. However, I'm sure it's nothing I can't live with, that we can't deal with together. After all, we're both adults—and as I said earlier, my house is plenty big enough for the both of us. Why don't we plan on driving out there later today? That way, you can take a look around, decide what bedroom you think would suit you best. Then we can start getting your things moved in."

"This is really happening, isn't it? We're actually going to get married, aren't we?" Caroline smiled falteringly, trying to make light of the matter. "Somehow, I keep expecting to wake up and find out it's all just a dream."

"I know. I feel the same way," Nick admitted, running one hand raggedly through his hair. "But, yes, it's real, and together we'll just have to try and make the best of it. And we will, Caroline. I promise you that." He paused, taking a deep breath, before he smiled down at her again—this time a roguish grin that, despite herself, managed somehow to set her pulse racing. "And now, I suppose we'd better get to work. I've got a ton of things to do in the lab if I'm going to bring your grandmother's secret youth formula to fruition.''

"If you don't mind, Nick, I think I'd like to be alone for a little while to try to come to grips with our situation, to get some perspective on it. So you go on. And when you're ready to take that drive out to your house, why don't you buzz my office? I'll have my secretary clear my calendar for the remainder of the day, so I'll be at your disposal.''

"Well, in spite of everything, I have to admit I like the sound of that,'' he drawled insolently, grinning wickedly at her once more, impervious to her sudden scowl and flush of embarrassment. "Oh, hell. Lighten up, Caro. After all, it isn't every day that a person gets engaged. Besides, it could be worse. It could be Otto the INS is attempting to deport!'' Otto Mueller was his stolid, heavyset assistant in the laboratory. Then, before Caroline realized what Nick intended, he bent his head to brush her lips quickly with his own. "Sorry. I just couldn't resist. I simply *had* to know whether or not you'd taste like a sweet roll!'' he insisted before grabbing his attaché and heading from Kate's office.

Caroline stood there staring after him, nonplussed, biting her tongue to hold back the question that had involuntarily sprung to it: *Well, do I?* Unwittingly, her hand flew to her mouth. Somehow, her lips felt warm from his kiss. At that realization, she shook her head resolutely, as though to clear it.

What was she thinking? Really, the man was impossible! Any concern and empathy she had thought he might have felt for her earlier had obviously been an attempt on his part to conceal his true self from her, in order that she would say yes to marrying him.

How could she go through with their wedding? Caroline asked herself, torn. Because how could she *not* go through with it? Her grandmother, father and Fortune Cosmetics were all counting on her. She couldn't let them down, couldn't turn her back on them and prove a disappointment to them, as her brother, Adam, had done.

No, like it or not, she had no choice but to wed Nick Valkov. She sighed heavily. This was not the marriage of her dreams, what she had envisioned since she was a little girl. She had hoped for a loving husband, children.

Her eyes strayed to the elegant marble pedestal that stood in one corner of her grandmother's office. From the column, a small, slender alabaster arm rose. Wrapped around its wrist was a sterling-silver heirloom baby bracelet composed of tiny beads and a delicate heart. It was quite valuable, as it was believed to have belonged to one of history's great queens. But that was not the reason why Caroline had always loved it. It was because, to her, it somehow symbolized all that life should be, the making of the proverbial happy home and hearth, the passing of the torch from one generation to the next.

She was twenty-nine years old—and she could hear her biological clock ticking away. How much time would she lose by marrying Nick Valkov, time she might have spent looking for a true husband who loved her and would give her children? How much time had she already wasted herself, burying herself in her work and cutting herself from all men? She had been a fool, Caroline realized now. But it was too late to go back; she could not relive the past.

She must, as her father had, set aside her own dreams for the good of the family. Thus resolved, she squared her shoulders determinedly and strode from her grandmother's office.

Four

When, late that afternoon, Nick finally rang her office, Caroline was actually relieved. She had both dreaded and anticipated his call all day, so she had hardly been able to concentrate on her work. As a result, she had got very little accomplished, and she knew there was no point in continuing to fritter away any more time at her desk.

"I'll come up to your office to get you," said Nick. "I think we need to be seen to be in contact with each other, so that if the INS starts nosing around, questioning employees here at Fortune Cosmetics, they'll at least discover *some* signs that we might have been having a discreet affair—and perhaps believe that we got more excited and careless as we moved toward marriage. So be sure your secretary's there."

"All right," Caroline agreed slowly, knowing his plan was logical but still reluctant to fall in with it. She had been an object of gossip at Fortune Cosmetics during her relationship with Paul Andersen, and she loathed the thought of becoming so again. She had worked hard to put the past behind her. "I'll see you in a few minutes, then." After disconnecting, instead of hanging up the receiver, she punched in her secretary's extension. "Mary, I've got those letters that needed my signature ready now, if you'd like to come in and get them."

"Great. I'll be right there," the young, bubbly secretary replied.

Moments later, Mary appeared in the doorway. Instead of handing her the letters right away, Caroline pretended to sort through all the papers on her littered desk, chatting with the secretary and feeling like a fool at deceptively delaying her until Nick arrived. Caroline was glad when he finally showed up.

"Caro baby...oh, I didn't realize you weren't alone, Ms. Fortune," he uttered contritely as he stuck his head inside the doorway, feigning momentary confusion and discomposure.

He did it so well, seemed so practiced at subterfuge, that for an instant, Caroline could not help but wonder if the INS really *was* right and if Nick really *was* a former KGB agent. Then she realized how ridiculous an idea that was.

Because if he were, he certainly wouldn't have come to the United States and taken a job as a chemist at a cosmetics company. He would surely have sought a position at something like an electronics or aircraft company, or as a government official or a politician, so he would have access to the kind of information that would be valuable on the open market—to foreign governments and terrorists.

While rival cosmetics companies might be interested in finding out that Fortune Cosmetics was going to call its new shade of red lipstick and matching nail polish Maraschino Cherry, Caroline simply couldn't imagine that anybody else would pay highly for that knowledge—or that it would attract the attention of a secret agent.

Taking a deep breath, she forced herself to play along with the game Nick had devised, acutely aware of the sudden speculation in Mary's bright eyes as she looked at the two of them.

"Nick...Dr. Valkov, I'll be right with you." Handing Mary the letters, Caroline said quickly, "Thank you, Mary. That'll be all," not having to fake the expression of embarrassment on her face.

"Yes, Ms. Fortune." The young secretary departed, firmly closing the door behind her, although not before casting from beneath her lashes an adoring, flirtatious glance of invitation at Nick—as though he were some rich, handsome, famous movie star or something, Caroline thought, disgusted and annoyed.

"Well, I don't think you have to worry about your plan not working, Nick," she declared acidly, by way of greeting. "I feel sure that by tomorrow afternoon, Mary will have spread the rumor all through the building that you and I are having an affair! Honestly, did you *have* to call me 'Caro baby'?"

"Of course." That impudent grin of his split his face, doing strange things to her insides. "That's what I'd call you if you and I really *were* involved together. I mean, I've heard Kyle and Allie both refer to you by the nickname Caro. I like it, actually—and it really would suit you just fine if you'd ever let your hair down—both figuratively *and* literally!" His eyes danced with mischief as he gazed at her assessingly. Then, shaking his head and shrugging nonchalantly at the reproving look she gave him in response, he continued. "Besides, what's a little more grist for the gossip mill, anyway? It's already churning overtime with the report that you gave Kyle the sack yesterday. Is that true?"

"Yes—and I guess with what Mary will have to tell tomorrow morning, everybody will soon be saying that Kyle's departure is somehow tied to our relationship!" The notion irritated Caroline no end. "And the truth is that Grandmother was right. He just wasn't cut out for the corporate life. And if we're going to make this marriage to save your hide work, I really *must* insist that you stop making these unflattering observations about my personal appearance and character. Just because I don't choose to dress like some flamboyant punk rocker and behave like a gregarious, glad-handing Pollyanna doesn't mean I am, in reality, the haughty, aloof Ice Queen that everybody at Fortune Cosmetics calls me behind my back!"

By now, Caroline was so wrought up that she was practically shouting—she, who never raised her voice, who always dealt with everyone and everything so coolly and calmly. She couldn't believe it. She didn't know what was the matter with her, how she had come to lose her temper so badly in the space of just a few minutes.

Adding to her mortification and outrage was the fact that Nick didn't look in the least perturbed by her outburst. Instead, his dark eyes gleamed with amusement—and something more—and his mouth was curved in a smile of what appeared to her, strangely, like satisfaction.

For the second time in as many days, she had to quell the urge that assailed her to box his ears and wipe the smirk clean off his face.

"Well, it would seem there is, indeed, fire beneath the ice," he drawled disconcertingly. "And to think that all this time, I thought you possessed a very slow-burning fuse, Caro. I stand corrected." Striding to her office closet, he opened the door and withdrew her coat, holding it out for her. "Shall we go, my fiery bride-to-be?"

Incensed and unnerved, Caroline opened her mouth to issue a caustic retort, then, with effort, closed it again, knowing instinctively that nothing she might say would put a dent in Nick's armor. He was obviously a master at the duel of wits between a man and a woman—and she was barely a novice. She couldn't possibly hope to compete with him in this arena.

That realization disturbed her. She was accustomed to being better than most at whatever she put her mind to. That in Nick Valkov she had perhaps met her match was an irksome thought.

Abruptly turning her back to him, she slid her arms into her coat, he wrapping his own arms around her as he helped her into it. For a moment, despite how she attempted to pull away from him, Nick held her close against his hard, lean body. Despite herself, the physical contact, the warmth of him, set her heart to hammering. He bent his head to her nape, inhaling deeply.

"Appassionato." He correctly identified the expensive Fortune perfume she wore. "A formula made up of jasmine, gardenias, lilies, roses, vetiver, musk and a few other intoxicating essences positively guaranteed to charm the savage beast." His voice was low and husky in her ear.

"Don't you mean 'soothe the savage beast'?" Caroline asked tartly.

"No, I don't." He released her then, sliding his hand under her elbow to escort her from the office. "It's still early enough that if we hurry, we'll miss most of the rush-hour traffic," he observed as they made their way past Mary—who watched them covertly from her desk—then into one of the elevators that would take them down to the parking garage. "We'll take my car," Nick announced peremptorily.

"No, there's no need for that," Caroline protested. "I can follow you in my own car out to your house. That'll save you from having to make an unnecessary trip back into town."

"I don't mind. Besides which, the drive will give us a chance to start getting better acquainted." After unlocking it, Nick opened the passenger door of his sleek black Mercedes-Benz to assist Caroline inside. Then, leaning over her, he fastened her seat belt for her. "I don't want anything to happen to you," he explained cockily. "Wives don't grow on trees, you know—and I'm afraid that the thought of winding up with somebody like Agnes Grimsby would make me thank the INS for deporting me!"

Agnes Grimsby worked in the company's cafeteria and was the female counterpart of Otto Mueller. Caroline couldn't help but laugh at the incongruous image of Agnes and Nick together.

"Actually, I think you and Agnes would make a lovely couple," she insisted, doing her best to keep a straight face as, after opening his own door, Nick slid into the seat beside her. "I'd be happy to hint to her that you're interested...."

"Don't even think about it—or else I'm going to make sure you wind up with dependable old Otto following you around like a faithful puppy." Punching the key into the ignition, Nick started the car, backing out from the parking space that was reserved for him. Some minutes later, the Mercedes-Benz was traveling along one of the freeways, heading west from the city. Nick turned on the radio, and classical music began to drift softly from the speakers. "So...what's your favorite color?" he queried.

"Lilac, why?"

"Because that might be one of the things the INS will ask us if they decide to investigate our marriage. Husbands and wives generally know little details like that about each other. My favorite color is blue, by the way. I smoke Player's cigarettes. I drink Stoly... Stolichnaya vodka," he clarified at her inquiring glance. "I like the ballet, snowy winters, moonlit walks along the lakeshore and—as you've probably no doubt guessed by now—classical music. When it comes to laboratories and chemicals, I'm the prover-bial whiz kid. I'm thirty-four years old, six-foot-one, and weigh a hundred and eighty pounds—most of it solid muscle, because I work out at a gym at least five times a week. Do you think you can remember all that?"

"I'll give it a shot. But honestly, Nick, I have to tell you that it sounds to me like you're providing me with a dossier, preparing me for some sort of spy mission. Are you *sure* you're not a former KGB agent?" Caroline was only half joking.

"Yes, I'm sure. When you've grown up the way I did—behind the Iron Curtain before it fell—you tend to take politics quite seriously. My country's come a long way in the past few years, but it's still got a long way to go. My job there was strictly of a civilian nature. So let me reassure you. You don't have to worry that you're about to embark upon some escapade more appropriate to a James Bond movie, Caro." Nick's voice was wry.

"I'm sorry. But I—I couldn't help but wonder. I mean, there must be *some* reason why the INS would have come to such a mistaken conclusion about you, which would lead them to want to deport you, Nick."

"Don't you think I have considered that? In fact, I've thought of nothing else since I opened that damned INS letter. I know I'm innocent of these shadowy allegations against me, so I have to believe there's something else at the bottom of this matter."

"Like what?"

"Like... maybe despite all our precautions, word has somehow leaked out about the secret youth formula. Even though it's strictly confidential at Fortune Cosmetics, there must be any number of people who have access to information about it, including assistants and secretaries. What I'm wondering now is if one of our competitors has somehow got wind of it... enough of a whiff, at any rate, that they figured out that removing a key element—meaning me— would represent a major setback to Fortune Cosmetics."

"Oh, Nick!" Caroline exclaimed, stricken. "Nothing like that had even occurred to me! I just can't imagine that anyone at the company would prove so untrustworthy. Actually, until this very moment, I've always thought grandmother's gone a trifle overboard when it comes to her fears about industrial espionage. But now...I don't know what to think. What if you're right? How could we find out? What could we do to try to protect ourselves from this kind of thing in the future? And what if our marriage simply leads whoever is behind this to target somebody else at Fortune Cosmetics?''

''Well, then at least we'll have some sort of an answer, won't we,'' Nick rejoined grimly. ''However, I wouldn't worry about it at the moment, Caro. Except for what's happened to me, there's no real reason at this point to suspect industrial espionage. I only mentioned it because I think we should at least bear it in mind as a possibility.''

He turned onto a secluded drive that wound through stands of trees toward the lake, pulling the car to a momentary halt before a big, rustic but beautiful house. To Caroline, it seemed a part of its surroundings, lightly shrouded with snow and ice, and glittering in the dusk like some kind of enchanted woodland palace.

''Here we are. Home. Do you like it, Caro?'' Nick asked softly, not understanding why he had paused here in the drive so she could see the house fully before going inside, why it was suddenly so important to him that she found it pleasing.

"Yes, I do...very much. It's just lovely...a dream house—but, quite frankly, not at all what I expected, Nick. I thought you'd have something...oh, I don't know...much more elegant and sophisticated, like your car, I guess."

"Ah, yes. But you see, that's only my public persona," he asserted, smiling. "I'm much different in my private life."

"Are you?"

"Yes. That's one of the things you'll discover about me...in time." He shifted the Mercedes-Benz and pulled around the drive, into the garage. Shortly afterward, he led Caroline into the house, flicking on lights as they went.

The interior surprised her as much as the exterior had. The great room soared to its heavy timber rafters, one whole wall nothing but windows that provided a magnificent view of the lake beyond. Snow white carpet stretched across the floor to kiss a towering fieldstone fireplace with a huge, unscreened hearth and oak logs piled high in the niche. From both sides of the room, open staircases rose to meet the upstairs balcony that ran along three walls above. Overstuffed, contemporary chairs and sofas mingled with antique armoires and tables, on which sat Tiffany lamps and Lalique vases. The latter were filled with fresh mixed flowers that Caroline knew, in the dead of winter, had to have come from a florist.

The entire room managed at once to be exquisite and yet invitingly comfortable. It was, she thought, startled, actually very much like her own apartment, very much the way she had always envisioned a real home of her own would be.

In that moment, strangely, she suddenly found it difficult to believe she and Nick were not really going to be married in any true sense of the word, that they were not going to be building a life here together, making children together.

Get a grip, Caro! she told herself sternly as she abruptly realized the direction her thoughts had taken. *This is purely a business arrangement, so don't go making a fool of yourself by starting to think it's anything else. Good heavens! Yesterday morning, you didn't even like Nick Valkov!*

"Here, let me take your coat, and then I'll show you around." Smoothly, Nick slipped her coat from her shoulders before conducting her on a tour of the premises.

These included a large, warm, welcoming country kitchen filled with plants, baskets and copper pots, a study where Nick obviously worked when at home, a library filled from floor to ceiling with books, and then four bedrooms upstairs—one of which was his own.

It was a wholly masculine room, dominated by a massive canopy bed, an armoire and a dresser, another large fireplace and Russian works of art.

Quickly, Caroline averted her gaze from the bed, having suffered another unbidden image of herself and Nick together, this time lying naked and entangled on the goose-down duvet.

As though he had read her mind, Nick drawled, "You are, of course, welcome to sleep here, if you wish."

"Ours is to be a marriage in name only," Caroline reminded him, knowing she was blushing again and grateful for the dim lamplight, which she hoped concealed her pink cheeks.

"Of course," he responded evenly, although she thought she saw a glimpse of regret in his eyes—which surprised her. After all, this morning he hadn't seemed too enthused about having her as his wife. "Still, you can't blame a guy for trying, can you? Which of the other bedrooms would you prefer, then?"

"I'll take the one at the other end of the hall." Caroline's gaze fell nervously before his eyes, which glittered mockingly, knowingly, and his mouth, which twisted in a grin of amusement.

"Naturally," he drawled dryly. "I'll get it ready for you tomorrow. Would you like me to install a dead bolt on the door, as well?"

"Actually," she said quietly, glancing up at him again then—earnestly, so he would know she was serious, "I *was* hoping you would prove gentleman enough that I wouldn't need to make such a request, Nick."

"I am—more's the pity. So you don't need to worry that after we're married, I won't keep my end of the bargain, Caro. Or that I'll fall on you like some ravaging beast one night when you least expect it. I won't—at least, not unless you want me to," he added insolently, grinning again. Then, as yet another blush stained her cheeks, he observed, "You're really not used to being teased by a man, are you. Somehow, I find that highly intriguing and most illuminating. I'm beginning to realize you're actually nothing at all like the woman I've always imagined you to be. Shall we go back downstairs now, have a little supper and a nightcap before I run you back to the office to pick up your car?"

"Oh, no. That's not necessary," she insisted quickly, her heart beating fast in her breast at his observations about her. He was very perceptive. She would have to be on her guard against him, Caroline realized. Otherwise, he would soon be tunneling his way beneath the defenses she had so carefully erected around her inner self, the barriers that shielded her heart. "Really. It's getting late, and you'll still have to come back here after dropping me off. I can grab a quick bite to eat on my way home."

"What? A greasy burger from some fast-food place? I don't think so. Forgive me for speaking so bluntly, Caro, but a body like yours deserves better." Nick's gaze roamed over her again appreciatively. He made a short *tsk*ing sound with his mouth. "I confess

I can already see that I might grow to regret this look-but-don't-touch marriage of ours. Oh, well. I'll just have to learn to live with it, I guess. Come on. My beef stroganoff is to die for.''

This last was not an idle boast, Caroline presently learned after they had gone downstairs into the kitchen. There, what was supposed to have been a "little supper" somehow turned into a rather grand and lengthy production, as though Nick were in no great hurry to get rid of her. In fact, Caroline thought, bewildered, he was behaving as though they were on a real date and he were doing his best to win her approval. And the more charming he acted, the more her pulse raced and the more she felt herself being enveloped by an indefinable sense of panic.

She tried to remind herself that this was the same man she had for ages thought of as being impossibly arrogant, domineering and insufferable, a man with highly archaic, Old World tendencies, which involved keeping a woman barefoot and pregnant. But it didn't help.

Nick's obviously mercurial moods, his light-hearted—clearly deliberately risqué—teasing, his intelligent conversation…all contrived to make Caroline feel as though she were being sucked helplessly into some dangerous whirlpool from which there was no escape. Despite all her worldly, sophisticated family background, she was out of her depth in this milieu, she reflected, dismayed. She hadn't had enough experience with men to know how to deal with one like Nick Valkov.

She wondered what motivated his attitude toward her, if his pleasantness and flirting were his way of attempting to seduce her. He had something of a reputation as a playboy at Fortune Cosmetics. Had he decided that the prospect of a prolonged period of celibacy held no appeal, after all? Finally, unable to restrain her curiosity any longer, she asked him outright why he was apparently putting his best foot forward where she was concerned.

"I thought I had made it clear to you earlier, Caro." With a pair of tongs, he expertly tossed the salad he was preparing—Russian dressing, of course, she noted. "Depending on the position the INS takes with regard to our marriage, we may be husband and wife for as much as a year—or even longer. And personally, I simply don't relish the idea of spending that much of my life in a veritable war zone. You know the old saying that a man's home is his castle? Well, it's true. And I want mine peaceful—not filled with hostilities. So, of course I've been trying my best to put you at ease toward that end. It seemed the only sensible course of action—and until now, I *had* flattered myself that I had something of a way with women. However, it would appear from your words that where you, at least, are concerned, I am failing miserably."

"No...it's not that. It's not that at all. I was just...puzzled, that's all."

"In what way?"

"Well, you've just never seemed quite so...oh, I can't explain it. You've just always struck me as being very—"

"Proud, egotistical, impatient, demanding and not a man to be ruled by a woman?" He laughed softly at her obvious surprise. "You see, I *do* know my own faults. Caro—the main one of which is that I don't suffer fools gladly." Taking up the beef stroganoff, he placed it on the table, which she had set earlier. "But you're not a fool. In fact, you're probably one of the smartest women I've ever had the pleasure to know, and whether you think so or not, I do respect that."

"But you'd rather I were stupid?"

"No, I wouldn't, actually. I prefer intelligent women. But intelligent women are usually also strong, stubborn, ambitious, independent women who have no tolerance or respect for weak men. Tell the truth, Caro," he prodded as he pulled out a chair for her. "Wouldn't you rather marry a man like me than some poor schmuck like Ernie Thompkins in the mail room?"

"Ernie's a very nice guy." Caroline deftly dodged the question.

"Yes, well, we all know where they finish up, don't we?" For a moment, she caught a flash of steel in Nick's eyes, so she knew with certainty that *he* would never end up in last place. He was too clever and determined for that. "And don't think I didn't notice how neatly you ducked out of answering me. I did. So be warned—you'll have to get up pretty early in the morning to put anything over on me, Caro."

"Why would I ever want to? I'm not a deceitful person, Nick, and if there's one thing I believe in, it's honesty in a relationship. And I'm sure you know why that is, too."

"Yes, word did get around the company about you and Paul Andersen." Nick dished up the salad, beef Stroganoff and crusty French bread he had prepared, then set her plate before her. After opening a bottle of Beaujolais from his small wine cellar, he poured her glass half full. "That must have hurt, stung your pride, broke your heart—knowing the guy was only marrying you for money."

"But isn't that one of the reasons why *you* agreed to wed me?"

Nick glanced at her sharply from beneath hooded eyes. "That's different. Ours is an arranged marriage, a business deal. I never led you on, pretended to love you in order to get you to a wedding altar. I find the fact that Andersen did despicable. Now, eat up. You're not your supermodel sister Allie, thank heavens. You don't have to run around looking like some gaunt refugee who just got off a raft from Robinson Crusoe's island."

"How can you say that? Allie's gorgeous!"

"So are you, Caro," Nick declared lightly, although his eyes were strangely now sober. "But I'm beginning to understand that you don't realize that. That ever since your disastrous affair with Andersen, you have had no sense whatsoever of your worth as a woman.''

Caroline didn't know how to reply to that. She wasn't accustomed to having a handsome man tell her she was attractive. Usually, she intimidated men. Or suspected they were only interested in her share of the Fortune riches.

Nick, however, didn't appear to be daunted by her in the least, and while it was true he was being paid a tidy sum to marry her, he wasn't going to gain access to any of her own personal wealth by the deed. So he had no need to pay her compliments.

To cover her confusion, she dug into the beef Stroganoff, finding it delicious. ''This is wonderful! Where did you learn how to cook?''

''Oh, when you're a single man who appreciates good food, you either dine out a lot or else you figure out how to fix it yourself. I chose the latter course.''

''You've never been married before, then?'' Caroline inquired, curious.

''No. This will be a first for me.''

''Me, too. I guess that's why—in addition to the circumstances themselves—it all seems so awkward and unnerving, so unreal.''

''Once we grow more accustomed to the idea, to each other, those feelings will pass, Caro. Then you'll undoubtedly turn into a nag who knows how to handle a rolling pin in more ways than one. I'll probably come home late one night to be cracked over the head by you for stopping off for a drink with the boys."

"No, you won't," Caroline stated firmly. "I've already told you I plan to interfere with your life as little as is humanly possible, Nick."

"Well, time will tell, won't it?" he remarked enigmatically.

After supper, Caroline insisted on helping clear away the dishes and clean up the kitchen. When that chore was almost done, Nick left her to complete it while he went into the great room to build a fire in the fireplace. It was blazing cheerfully by the time she joined him, and he had the stereo playing quietly, the strains of Tchaikovsky's *Sleeping Beauty* wafting from the speakers.

Nick himself sat on the floor, near the big, square coffee table in front of the fireplace, his back against one of the twin sofas. Two of the Tiffany lamps glowed softly, and two glasses of wine sat on the coffee table.

It was the seduction scene from any number of movies, Caroline thought, swallowing hard. And he was more than qualified for the leading-man role.

Earlier, before fixing supper, he had taken off his suit jacket and tie, loosened his collar and rolled up his shirtsleeves. Now, as he lounged on the floor, his long, powerful legs stretched out before him, she was forced to admit to herself that no matter what she thought about him personally, she still found him terribly attractive physically.

He had his head laid back upon the sofa; his eyes were closed, and he was smoking a cigarette, obviously reveling in the music. Instinctively, she knew this was how he spent many a long winter evening when he wasn't otherwise engaged.

"Nick, it's getting late. I should be getting home," she said.

"Yes, I know that's what you'd like, Caroline." His voice was low, silky—like the satisfied purring of a predatory panther—and he didn't even bother to open his eyes to look at her when he spoke. "But I'm afraid you're going to be forced to spend the night here with me instead."

At that wholly unexpected announcement, Caroline could only stare at him wide-eyed, abruptly horrified, panic-stricken, her heart pounding in her throat, her palms sweating. Given its size and location, Nick's house had to sit on at least a couple of acres of land, she judged, so there were no near neighbors she could run to for assistance. And since he had insisted on driving her out here, she had no car of her own. She thought he must have planned that from the very beginning, so she would be trapped here alone with him, unable to escape.

No, surely, he could not be serious about keeping her here, she tried to reassure herself. Surely, he must know there were laws against rape in the United States.

But Nick was Russian, from a country where women did not have as many rights and freedoms, as much protection under the law, as they did here in America—for whatever that was worth. Because even here, the rape statistics were terrible—worse even than the officially recorded figures, since many women, out of fear and shame, chose not to report the brutal, degrading crime against them. Perhaps because of that, Nick thought he would not be punished if he coerced her compliance.

Caroline didn't know what to say, what to do. As she studied his carelessly sprawled figure, his arms and legs corded with muscle, she knew she hadn't a prayer of fighting him off. Even if she ran upstairs and locked herself in one of the bedrooms, there was nothing to prevent him from simply breaking down the door to get at her.

"Nick, you can't honestly mean to keep me here against my will, to—to force yourself on me." Somehow, she managed to choke out the words, her hands clenching into fists at her sides, as though she were already preparing to do battle with him.

At that statement, his eyes flew open wide, and as his gaze took in her ashen face, her saucerlike eyes filled with apprehension, he growled harshly what she suspected was a very foul curse word, although she couldn't be certain, because he spoke it in Russian. Then, without warning, he leaped to his feet and strode toward her determinedly, his face grim, a muscle throbbing in his taut, set jaw.

Utterly terrified then, Caroline screamed and turned to flee. But he caught her before she was even halfway across the room. Frantic, she struck out at him wildly, hammering her fists against his broad chest, shrieking and sobbing protests, while he gripped her upper arms tightly, refusing to release her and still snarling at her furiously in Russian.

Then finally, after several long, awful minutes, it dawned on Nick that in the heat of the moment, he had lapsed into his native language, so she couldn't understand him, and he abruptly switched to English.

"Caroline, stop it! *Stop it!* Stop fighting me!" he snapped angrily, giving her a small, rough shake as she hit him in the chest again. "I'm not going to hurt you, damn it! My God! What in the hell kind of man do you think I am, anyway? I only meant that even if you held a gun to my head, I simply *couldn't* take you back into town tonight. Have you even looked outside, for pity's sake?"

She hadn't, but she did then, glancing out the huge bank of windows and gasping at the sight that met her frightened, tearful eyes. It was snowing—hard—and obviously had been for quite some time. His long, serpentine driveway was probably buried by now.

"I can't get my snowplow out there until tomorrow morning, when it will be light enough to see what I'm doing," he told her.

"Oh, Nick, I am *so* sorry," Caroline said weakly, in a very small, mortified voice. "I feel like such a fool...so embarrassed and ashamed. I thought—I thought—"

"I know what you thought, damn it! It's *why* you thought it that has me so damned mad! Is that really what you think of me, Caroline? That I'm the kind of man who would rape you, for God's sake!"

"No...no, of course not. It's just that...well, you're quite big and strong, extremely masculine and—and foreign...with what I've always thought of as Old World patterns of male thinking. And so when you said what you did, I—I just jumped to the wrong conclusion, that's all. I'm so sorry...." Her voice trailed away, and she bit her lower lip contritely, unable to meet his eyes, her own brimming again with tears. Then, after a moment, she continued quietly.

"You don't know, Nick—you *can't* know, because I never told anyone—but the night I confronted Paul about him wanting to wed me only because of my money, he went crazy, and he...attacked me. He'd been drinking pretty heavily that evening, so I don't know what he was thinking. I mean, it wasn't as though we...hadn't already slept together, or that forcing himself on me would cause me to change my mind and marry him, after all. At any rate, if he hadn't been so drunk, I wouldn't have been able to fend him off. But even though I managed to get him out of my apartment, I still felt so stupid and humiliated afterward at being so misled by him that I—I just couldn't bring myself to trust any man enough again to let him get close to me.''

''Shhh. It's all right, Caro. Really. I understand,'' Nick crooned comfortingly as her tears spilled from her eyes at last.

He drew her into his arms then, holding her close against his whipcord body. During their struggle, her hair had come loose from its stylish French twist, and now he gently tugged the rest of the pins from it, combed it with his fingers, so it fell around her shoulders in a thick, silly sable mass. Somehow in the process, he managed to remove her tortoiseshell glasses, too, laying them aside on a nearby table.

In that instant, instinctively seeking reassurance and solace, Caroline didn't object to his actions. Lost in the pain of her past, she was hardly even aware of them. But after a time, she eventually did begin to grow acutely conscious of how she was pressed against Nick's warm, hard body, of the strong, steady beat of his heart against her ear, of how he stroked her unbound hair and her back soothingly, and of the fact that although he truly intended only to offer her consolation, he had nevertheless become aroused by her proximity.

Involuntarily, Caroline glanced up at him then, her brown eyes startled and momentarily confused, her mouth slightly parted in a small gasp of surprise. As Nick's own nearly black eyes met hers, they abruptly darkened, glittering like obsidian as he stared down at her. Then he swore softly, and before she realized his intention, his lips swooped to capture her own.

In the beginning, his kiss was tentative, tender. But when, taken unaware, Caroline did not demur, Nick's mouth grew harder, hungrier, more demanding. His tongue traced the outline of her lips before compelling them to part and thrusting inside, tasting and taunting. Unbidden, Caroline felt a sudden surge of longing and excitement sweep through her, setting her aflame. Of their own volition, her arms crept up to wind around his neck, and his own arms tightened around her, his hands tangling in her hair.

In some dazed corner of her mind, she reflected dimly that he had chosen his profession aptly, because there was definitely strong chemistry at work between them . . . roiling like some combustible liquid in a beaker heating over a Bunsen burner, about to explode. But at that thought, Caroline recognized that by not protesting, by letting Nick kiss and caress her like this, she was undoubtedly giving him the wrong impression: that she was his for the taking—both tonight and for the duration of their marriage.

Abruptly, she broke away from him, trembling from the yearnings he had wakened inside her, her knees so unexpectedly weak and fluid that she was compelled to lay one hand on the nearby table to steady herself. The other flew involuntarily to her mouth, moist and heated from his kisses.

"Nick, it really *is* getting late, so if you don't mind, I'd like to go to bed now," she told him breathlessly—then flushed furiously as she realized what she had inadvertently said, the unintentional double entendre of her words.

"Hmmm. That sounds like a real good idea to me," he drawled lazily in response, his eyes drowsy beneath half-shuttered lids, an enigmatic smile curving his lips.

"That is *not* what I meant—and what's more, you know it!"

"Do I, Caro baby? And are *you* sure that's not what you meant?" His eyes gleamed wickedly now, and his smile broadened as she nodded tersely before kneeling to retrieve her hairpins scattered on the floor, then rising to pick up her glasses from the table. "Ah, well. Never let it be said that I don't know how to accept defeat gracefully. I guess I'll just have to comfort myself with the fact that I at least got to see you with your hair down and your glasses off—and that wasn't a shabby consolation prize, by any means."

He escorted her upstairs to the bedroom she had selected for herself and gave her one of his shirts to sleep in. Since she knew she'd have to wear her winter-white wool suit again in the morning, Caroline hung it up in the closet carefully after she had taken it off. Then she bathed in the sunken tub of the bathroom that adjoined her bedroom and washed her lingerie out in the sink, draping it over the towel rack to dry. Nick's shirt was too big for her, hanging almost to her knees, the sleeves so long that she had to roll them up.

She was just fixing to get into bed when he knocked gently on her closed door. When she responded, Caroline only cracked it open, uncomfortably cognizant of the fact that she was stark naked beneath his shirt. Nick's gaze traveled the length of her admiringly, lingering on her long, bare legs, and then on the open collar that displayed a good deal of her skin—not to mention the pulse fluttering erratically at the hollow of her throat—before coming to rest on her face.

"I . . . ah . . . just wanted to check in on you before I went to bed, see if there was anything else you needed," he explained.

"No, thank you. There's nothing. I'm fine." Self-consciously, Caro drew the open collar edges of the shirt together, wondering anxiously if, in the glowing lamplight, he could actually see her nude body through the fine white cambric.

"Good. Well, if you happen to change your mind, you know where to find me," Nick said, both of them highly aware that his words held a double meaning. "Good night, Caro. Sweet dreams."

"Good night, Nick."

Caroline shut the door firmly, intensely conscious of the fact that he was still standing out in the hall, waiting to see whether or not she pushed the lock into place. If she did, he would know she didn't trust him to keep his word. If she didn't, he might perceive it as an invitation, she thought. Torn, she didn't know what to do. So it was much to her relief that after a moment, she heard him laugh softly in understanding of her predicament.

"Lock it, Caro, if it makes you feel better." Then he padded silently down the hall.

She climbed into bed, but despite her mental exhaustion born of her extremely unsettling day, Caroline found she still couldn't get to sleep and lay awake until the wee hours, tossing and turning restlessly.

She remembered the feel of Nick's mouth on hers, the swift, fiery response he had ignited in her. And she told herself fiercely that if she had one single ounce of common sense at all, she would back out of their arranged marriage first thing tomorrow morning—before it was too late.

Five

In the morning, Caroline discovered that it was already too late to change her mind, that her chance to call off the wedding had already been lost—if indeed she had ever truly had one at all.

She thought that perhaps she had not. Her conscience and her loyalty to her family had always dictated her actions—and now was no exception to that rule. So despite that after grooming and dressing herself, she went downstairs resolved to inform Nick that she could not go through with their marriage, the words died upon her lips as soon as she saw him.

He wore an elegant black Armani suit; its jacket and his foulard tie were tossed over one of the chairs at the kitchen table, upon which lay a pair of gold Cartier cuff links. The collar of his fine white Turnbull & Asser shirt was open, and his sleeves were rolled up, displaying his strong forearms and the gold Rolex watch that encircled his left wrist. His thick, dark hair, combed back in neat wings, shone glossily, as though it were newly washed and still damp.

Despite herself, Caroline felt her heart lurch in her breast at the sight of him, and she thought that nobody should look so good in the morning.

Nick must have risen at least two hours before she had, she realized, because as she glanced out the wide bank of windows, she observed that the driveway was freshly plowed. In addition, he had breakfast ready and waiting for her on the kitchen table: omelets, Canadian bacon, fruit, croissants and hot coffee.

"Good morning, Caro." He smiled as he greeted her and, taking her unaware as he had last night, leaned over to brush her mouth with his own, as though they were already husband and wife and this were their usual morning ritual. "Did you sleep well?"

"Yes," she lied, not wanting him to know how she had lain awake until the early hours, tossing and turning restlessly—and thinking of him. She should tell him right off—straight out—that she had decided not to go through with their marriage, she told herself sternly. But to her dismay, as she looked at him, the words somehow stuck in her throat.

"Sit down, baby." Throwing a kitchen towel carelessly over his shoulder, Nick pulled out a chair at the table for her. "Are you hungry?"

"Yes, I am." To her surprise, Caroline found that she actually was, although she did not normally eat a big breakfast. "But you didn't have to fix all this, Nick. Really, I generally just grab a cup of coffee and a piece of toast in the mornings."

"I suspected as much," he replied. "However, food is like a fine wine or a good woman. It should be enjoyed and appreciated. We will therefore make every attempt to avoid eating breakfast on the run in our home."

Caroline was so nonplussed by this last comment that she didn't know how to respond. On the one hand, he appeared, however pleasantly, to be issuing a wholly dictatorial command and fully expecting that since he was a man—and, because of that, the natural, undisputed head of the household—his word would be obeyed as law. That notion filled her with indignation.

On the other hand, however, it had not escaped her notice that his statement had also contained words like *we* and *our home*. And although she insisted to herself that that meant nothing, had merely been a figure of speech, Caroline still could not repress the strange, unexpected thrill that shot through her, the sudden, wild hope that leaped in her breast.

Was he, in essence, trying to hint that he intended theirs to be a real marriage, after all? She didn't know, was afraid to ask.

At last, torn between her principles and her longings, and not wanting to start an argument at the breakfast table, she contented herself with answering, "Yes, Nick," wondering uncomfortably if with those two simple words, she had just betrayed every feminist tenet in the entire world.

Adding to this sense of conflict was the fact that upon hearing her reply, Nick smiled at her with both approval and satisfaction, as though she were a puppy who had successfully complied with its master's command. Caroline almost expected him to reach over and pat her on the head. She thought that if he did, he was shortly going to have egg all over his face—literally. Fortunately—and she had the oddest sensation that he had somehow read her mind in this regard—he did nothing so untoward but diligently applied himself to the meal instead.

"Are you planning to continue to do all the cooking after we're married, Nick?" Caroline asked, curious, as she, too, attacked her plate.

"No. Since we both work, I thought we'd share all the household chores equally—except that I won't expect you to mow the lawn in the summer or plow snow from the driveway in the winter."

"Well, that's real big of you!" she retorted dryly.

"Yes, I certainly thought so." Nick grinned impudently at her scowling face. "Do you know how many women till the fields of Russia?"

"Plenty of them, no doubt—since their husbands are probably passed out in a corner somewhere, sleeping off the ill effects of a drunken vodka binge!"

Nick laughed out loud at that. "Let me set your mind at ease, baby. While there are, indeed, some things I perhaps enjoy to excess, vodka isn't one of them." His eyes raked her licentiously, making his meaning plain and her pulse race. She could feel the hot color that crept into her cheeks. "Do you want butter or jelly on your croissant?"

"Butter." Caroline thought she should have known better than to try to match wits with him. He was always one step ahead of her, it seemed. And where she was concerned, that was rare for a man. Only Paul had managed to fool her, because she had loved him. She mustn't make that same mistake with Nick; she must remain on her guard and not allow her emotions to overwhelm her good judgment. "Why do you keep calling me that—baby, I mean?"

"Because that's what you're going to be this morning: my baby."

"I—I don't understand...."

"Well, then, let me make it clear to you. We're going to get married today, before we go into the office." Casually, Nick buttered her croissant, as though oblivious of the effect his words had upon her.

"*What?*" she cried, stricken.

"Caro..." He laid down his knife, wiped his hands on his linen napkin, then continued as patiently as though speaking to a child. "Your secretary saw us leave together yesterday afternoon. You spent the night here with me last evening. You've seen that I don't bite. So there's no reason for us to wait...for you to be exposed to any speculative or unsavory rumors on the job. If we go into work this morning and announce that we're married, all the gossip will center on that. We'll be congratulated for being so clever at concealing our relationship and snatching each other up."

Deep down inside, Caroline knew he was right, that his logic was irrefutable. Still, feeling the same sense of panic that had engulfed her last night, she protested. "Oh, Nick, I don't know. This is all so sudden. I'm—I'm just not sure I'm ready."

"Waiting a few more days isn't going to rid you of that uncertainty, baby. You had a bad experience with Andersen, and it's left you distrustful of all men. You've admitted that yourself. So what you're feeling has nothing to do with me personally, but with men in general. Our marriage will probably actually be good for you, Caro. You'll have a chance to live in close proximity with a man—with me—to experience a relationship without being pressured by societal expectations and emotional commitment. It'll give you the opportunity to learn that all men are *not* like Andersen and so that not all of your relationships with a man will follow the same grievous pattern."

"I thought you were a doctor of chemistry—not of psychology, Nick," Caroline observed stiffly, even though she knew in her heart that he had properly diagnosed what ailed her and prescribed what seemed an appropriate medicine.

"Chemistry is my chosen profession, yes. But that doesn't preclude my having an astute grasp of human nature, baby. So make up your mind—and then let's have no more discussion about this. Do you want to marry me or not?"

Here was her chance to escape, Caroline thought, her heart pounding. She had only to answer no. "Yes," she heard herself say instead.

"Good. Now finish your breakfast, and then we'll go."

When they were done eating, they cleared the table together, scraping the dishes and loading them into the dishwasher. Then, after rolling down his sleeves, Nick inserted his cuff links into his French cuffs, arranged his tie and shrugged on his suit jacket. He assisted her into her camel wool coat, put on his own heavy black topcoat and picked up both his briefcase and her own. After that, he flicked off the lights.

In the semidarkness of the kitchen, illuminated now only by the wintry gray light that filtered in through the uncurtained windows, he caught Caroline's chin in his hand, tilting her face up to his. "Poor baby." He smiled down at her gently, ruefully. "You look just like a lamb being led to slaughter. Do you really find me such an ogre as that?"

"No," she admitted softy, startled and touched by the kindness and comprehension she saw in his eyes. "Nick, before we go, I just want to tell you that although I know I'm not the wife you would have chosen for yourself, I'll at least try to be a good one to you for however long we're married."

"And I will be a good husband to you, Caroline. I understand and appreciate the sacrifice you're making for me, and you'll never have cause to regret this day, I swear."

Because Minnesota was a northern state, accustomed to long, hard, cold winters, the Twin Cities were well equipped to deal with even the worst snowfalls and did so efficiently. The plows had been out early that morning, so the freeway into Minneapolis was clear, and presently, Nick was pulling the car to a halt at the courthouse. He shut off the ignition, then turned to Caroline.

"Are you ready?" he asked, smiling at her encouragingly.

She took a deep breath. "Yes."

"No, you're not, actually. . . not quite."

Then, before she realized what Nick intended, he leaned over, caught hold of her hair wrapped up in its customary French twist, and began to tug the pins from it, so it spilled down below her shoulders in a long, shining tangle of rich sable.

"Nick! Nick, what are you doing?" Caroline cried, aghast, attempting unsuccessfully to make him stop.

"I don't like your hair that way, so I'm fixing it," he stated coolly, calmly ignoring her protests and struggle against him.

She tried to seize the pins from his grasp, but, pressing the button on his automatic window, he hurled them out into the parking lot. After that, he snatched her tortoiseshell glasses from her slender, finely sculpted nose. Holding them up to his eyes, he drawled, "Just as I thought. You don't really need these to see at all. Why, if these are prescriptive lenses, I'll eat my lab coat." Then, to her mortification and outrage, he pitched her glasses into the parking lot, as well.

Caroline would have scrambled from the car to retrieve them, but before she could get her door open, an automobile happened along, its right front tire running right over her glasses, crushing them. "My God. I do *not* believe what you just did." She stared at Nick as though she had never really looked at him before, shocked and stricken. "Why did you do it?"

"Because you've got gorgeous hair—it reminds me of Russian sable, thick, sleek and so incredibly soft and touchable—and big, beautiful brown eyes that are like molasses melting over a flame. I want to see your hair and eyes, Caro. As your husband—which I *will* be in just a few short minutes—I have that right. And since I didn't think you'd change your appearance for me, I took it upon myself to do it for you. Now you look the way a woman *should*—lovely, feminine, vulnerable and inviting—the way I want my bride to look. Shall we go?"

No matter how sorely provoked she might be, Caroline realized there was no point in arguing with Nick. Despite his claim to the contrary, he had had no right to do what he had done. Still, his words about her hair and eyes had thrilled her, flattered her, appeasing her as much as his actions had angered her.

She nodded tersely. "Yes, let's get this over with."

Although there was normally a waiting period, it turned out the presiding judge was a friend of the Fortune family, and was glad to issue a waiver. After that, the entire ceremony took less than a quarter of an hour. Once they were husband and wife, Nick caught hold of Caroline, drew her to him and kissed her lingeringly, thoroughly, his tongue following the curve of her mouth before insinuating itself inside. When he finally released her, she was faint and trembling with arousal. She marveled that he had only to kiss her to make her feel so. She had never felt like this with Paul.

"Come on, Mrs. Valkov." Nick's voice startled her from her dazed reverie. "Time to go to work."

Mrs. Valkov were the only two words that registered. Unconsciously, she glanced down at her left hand. Yesterday on his lunch hour, Nick had bought her a set of wedding rings. Caroline had not expected that. If she had given the matter any thought at all, she had vaguely imagined he would bestow a plain gold band upon her. But now, the resplendent rings—exquisite, lavish with diamonds—glittered up at her, letting her know this was no dream, that she truly *was* Ms. Fortune no longer, but Mrs. Valkov instead.

"Caro?"

"Yes, Nick, I'm coming." *Good heavens,* Caro thought even as she spoke, *I must be out of my mind to have gone through with this. I sound like some poor woman with no will of her own. "Yes, Nick" this and "Yes, Nick" that. I'm in a state of shock. That's what it is.*

But it was not her, but Kate, Jake and Sterling whom that condition more appropriately described when Nick and Caroline finally arrived at Fortune Cosmetics.

"What?" Kate exclaimed upon learning the news of their marriage. Staring at the two of them, her mouth agape, she abruptly sat down so hard in her desk chair that the gold charm bracelet she always wore jingled like Christmas bells. The bracelet had been given to Kate by her late husband, Ben, and with the birth of each child and grandchild in the family, a new charm had been added, so that the bracelet was now quite heavy and valuable. "What do you mean...you got married this morning? For Pete's sake, Caroline, what in the world were you thinking of? You're a Fortune, by God! My eldest granddaughter!" Kate's blue eyes snapped sparks of fury, and her cheeks were flushed. "You deserved a huge, splendid wedding—not some ten-minute trip to the courthouse, as though this were some hole-in-the-corner affair!"

"Well, isn't it?" Nick asked sharply, wholly unintimidated by Kate's wrath. "This is *our* marriage—

Caro's and mine—and we did what we thought was best under the circumstances.''

"Best for *you,* you mean!" Jake growled, siding with his mother and glaring at Caroline and Nick. "You *knew* that one of the things that Sterling was doing this week was drafting a prenuptial agreement, so my daughter's personal wealth would be safe!"

At Jake's insulting intimation, Nick swore softly, viciously, in Russian—the same words Caroline thought she had heard him speak last night, so she knew he was furious. "I don't want any of Caro's damned money!" he retorted hotly in English, a muscle flexing in his hard, set jaw. "Because of a number of extremely smart investments I've made over the years, I have plenty of my own, thank you very much! So I have every intention of signing whatever papers you want me to, Jake. You just send them down to the lab whenever you're ready!"

"I expect you to keep your word about that, Nick!" Jake asserted fiercely.

"Dad...Dad, please," Caroline entreated, upset by the argument, even though she knew her father was only trying to protect her. "I know you're mad, but Nick wouldn't steal my money. He's not that kind of a man."

Jake snorted derisively. "I'll remind you, pumpkin, that that's *exactly* what you said about Paul Andersen—and look how disastrous that affair turned out!"

"Don't you even think about dragging that slimy snake into this, Jake!" Nick hissed, his dark eyes narrowed. "Paul Andersen is a contemptible fool! Besides which, I'll remind *you* that it was your and Kate and Sterling's idea for Caroline and me to get married in the first place. But just because I permitted the three of you to arrange our marriage doesn't mean I intend to let you run it! Caro and I are perfectly capable of managing our own affairs."

"Perhaps you're right, Nick," Kate declared unexpectedly, her eyes now gleaming intensely with curiosity and fascination as she gazed thoughtfully at the bride and groom.

It had not escaped Kate's notice that despite the fact that Caroline and Nick were not in love and had been wed barely an hour, they nevertheless seemed already to have formed a solid partnership. They had banded together to justify their impetuous action of visiting the courthouse this morning, and each was defending the other's character, as well.

Further, Caroline's left hand sported a set of diamond wedding rings that any female would have envied—and that Nick need not have purchased, either. Nor had it eluded the older woman's observation that for the first time in more than five years, her granddaughter had appeared at work with her hair down and without those ridiculous tortoiseshell glasses she always insisted upon wearing.

Caroline actually looked this morning like the beautiful young woman she was, Kate thought as she studied her granddaughter fondly. The older woman could not help but believe Nick had been responsible for this welcome change. All in all, her scheme looked to be off to a great start, Kate decided, secretly as pleased as punch now that her ire over their having taken matters into their own hands had abated.

"I agree that we three have no right whatsoever to meddle in your and Caroline's business, Nick," she noted briskly. "However, I would be lying if I said I wasn't disappointed not to be able to give Caroline the lovely send-off she deserves. So perhaps *you'll* indulge *me* by agreeing to keep your marriage as quiet as possible for the time being. That way—even though it may be a few months later—we can still plan a big wedding ceremony and neither of you will have missed out on what ought to be one of the most wonderful, memorable events of any person's life—second only to the birth of children. What do you say, Nick?"

He glanced at Caroline silently, then back at Kate. "That'll be fine—and I know I speak for both of us when I say how much we appreciate both your offer and your understanding, Kate."

"Good. Now, in the meanwhile, why don't you and Caroline take the remainder of the week off, have a short honeymoon together? I'll have my secretary make you a reservation, why don't I?" Kate suggested, going on to propose a quiet but lovely place across the Canadian border, which she thought would be an ideal location for a honeymoon. "You can fly up in the corporate jet, and you'll be there in no time at all."

"Thank you, Grandmother," Caroline said warmly. For although the prospect of going off somewhere alone with Nick, ostensibly for a honeymoon, unsettled her, she was glad to escape from the inevitable gossip that was bound to circulate at Fortune Cosmetics, no matter how quiet she and Nick attempted to keep their marriage. "If that's all, then Nick and I will go on now to make arrangements to keep things running smoothly in our departments during our absence."

"Fine." Kate nodded approvingly. "You do that. I'll see you both later."

Once the newlyweds had departed, Jake turned to his mother, frowning. "What are you thinking of, Mother? You're positively beaming now—when, earlier, you were fuming. And you all but came right out and gave Caroline and Nick your blessing. Do you believe that was wise? After all, other than what we discovered during our background check of him, what do we really know about Nick? What if the INS is right and he really *is* a former KGB agent? What if he decides not to keep his word and refuses to sign the prenuptial agreement?"

"He isn't. He won't."

"How can you be so certain, Kate?" Sterling spoke for the first time.

"Call it women's intuition, if you like. But I know. I'm sure. Didn't you notice the change in Caroline?"

"Well . . . yes, now that you mention it, there *was* something different about her," Jake replied slowly. "Like maybe she had on our forthcoming shades of makeup for spring or something. I do remember thinking she looked unusually attractive this morning."

"Yes," Sterling agreed. "So do I."

Kate scowled momentarily at both men. "The two of you wouldn't see a grizzly coming until it jumped up and bit you on the butt! Open your eyes, damn it! Caroline looked different because she didn't have her hair done up in a French twist and she wasn't hiding behind those big glasses she doesn't need to begin with. And despite the fact that she was a little nervous—as any new bride is—she was *not* unhappy. She had the unmistakable glow of a woman falling in love. Only she doesn't know it yet, so mind . . . you're not to say anything to her! Or to Nick, either. Because unless I miss my guess—and I so very seldom do, you know—he's as moonstruck as she is and perhaps not quite so ignorant of the fact. You mark my words, both of you. This marriage is going to turn out to be one of the best things I ever arranged! Why, I'm willing to wager that I get at least two grandchildren out of the deal, if not more!" Kate chortled gleefully at the thought. "Now, shoo! I've got honeymoon reservations to make and a wedding to start planning!"

Shaking their heads, bemused by her behavior, Jake and Sterling left her office—neither man daring to voice to the other the idea each harbored in his mind: that perhaps Kate was at last getting senile in her old age.

Kate, guessing what they were thinking, snorted scornfully to herself as they closed the door behind them. *Men!* she thought ruefully. They just never had a clue about anything, the poor darlings. Why, if she had her way, women would not only be running corporations—they'd be running the world!

Six

True to her word, Kate had placed the Fortune corporate jet at Caroline and Nick's disposal. A limousine, also provided by Caroline's grandmother, had ferried them to the airport. Another had collected them at their journey's end and carried them here, to the Maplewood Lodge.

It was a beautiful, rustic retreat, set on the shores of a lake, amid a forest of maples. Instead of rooms, there were individual cabins, and it seemed to Caroline as the limousine lurched along the dirt trail rough with ice and snow that she and Nick had been assigned the most isolated and secluded of these.

"Grandmother must have come up here in the summer, when I'll bet this place is just gorgeous," Caroline remarked as she glanced out the tinted windows of the car, to which the lightly falling snow stuck briefly before being melted by the heater. "It probably didn't even occur to her that it wouldn't be quite the same in the winter."

"It's still lovely," Nick said softly. "It reminds me of Russia."

"You must miss your own country a lot."

"Yes—but not enough to go back there permanently. And now, thanks to you, I won't have to. I know my motive for wedding you was pretty damned selfish, Caro. But still, I'll always be grateful for what you did for me." His dark eyes appraised her warmly, so she blushed.

"Think nothing of it. Really. From my point of view, it was the only thing to do to save Grandmother's secret youth formula. So my motive was pretty selfish, too, Nick."

With a jolt caused by the rutted trail, the limousine at last rolled to a halt in front of their cabin. The driver got out to open their car door, while the bellboy who had accompanied them from the lodge disappeared into the cabin. Taking Caroline's hand, Nick helped her from the limousine. Then, before she realized his intention, he swept her up in his strong arms to carry her across the yard and then the threshold of the cabin.

"Nick! Put me down, Nick!" she squealed, mortified by the wide grins that split the faces of the limousine driver and the bellboy as they watched her futile struggle to free herself.

"Hush, Caro," Nick demanded. "And stop pounding me, for heaven's sake! I'm only doing my duty as your new husband." Inside the cabin, he finally set her on her feet, grinning as hugely as the other two men as he gazed down at her. His hand came up, gently brushing the sprinkling of snow from her hair. "A groom's supposed to carry his bride across the threshold—or am I wrong about that being an American wedding custom?"

"No, you're right. I...ah...just forgot about it, that's all," Caroline said lamely. For the truth was that since theirs was an arranged marriage, she hadn't been expecting him to follow tradition. But as she was beginning to learn, there was nothing about Nick that she could take for granted. He continually surprised her.

While the limousine driver brought in their luggage and the groceries they had bought on their way to the lodge, the bellboy opened the curtains and turned on the furnace to warm the chilly cabin. Caroline stripped off her coat and gloves and took stock of her surroundings.

The cabin's interior was not nearly as rustic as the exterior. In keeping with its backwoods theme, the furnishings were an eclectic mixture of primarily English and French Country; nevertheless, they were luxurious, reminding her of Nick's house. Comfortable love seats flanked the fieldstone fireplace that soared to the heavy timber rafters. Antique cupboards, sideboards and tables were scattered throughout. Ornate rugs lay upon the hardwood floor. To one side of the living room was a small kitchen. Through a door on the opposite side of the room were the bedroom and bath.

By now, Nick had taken care of tipping the limousine driver and the bellboy, and they had departed, leaving the newlyweds alone together.

"Nick!" Caroline called out to him as she stared at the bedroom dominated by another fireplace, a huge, pinewood armoire and dresser, and a brass canopy bed covered with a beautiful handmade quilt in the wedding-ring pattern. "Nick! I think there's been some mistake...that we must have been assigned to the wrong cabin."

"Why's that?" he asked as he joined her.

"Well, look. There's—there's only this one bedroom. That just can't be right. Grandmother knows the circumstances of our marriage. That being the case, she would surely have arranged for a two-bedroom cabin. You'd better phone the front desk and tell them."

"Tell them what, Caro? That even though we're newlyweds, we're not happy with the honeymoon cabin? Because that's what the bellboy told me this cabin is. Look outside." He motioned toward the windows, through which she could see that dusk had fallen and that the snow was coming down harder now. "Do you really want to go back out in that, baby? And what if the INS starts nosing around, sends somebody up here as part of their investigation of our marriage? Do you want them to find out we complained to the front desk on our wedding night and moved out of the honeymoon cabin into a two-bedroom one?''

"No, of course not," she answered slowly, realizing how that would look to the INS.

"Then let's just make the best of the situation, all right? I'll sleep on one of the love seats or something.''

"That—that won't be very comfortable for you.'' Caroline pointed out this fact reluctantly, hoping he wasn't going to interpret her words as an invitation to bed down with her. To make sure he didn't, she continued. "I'm smaller than you. It only makes sense that I sleep on the love seat.''

"No.'' He shook his head. "I appreciate the offer, but I'm afraid chivalry demands that *I* be the one to make do without a bed. But don't worry. I'll manage somehow. Now, what do you say to our getting unpacked and then rustling up something to eat?''

"That sounds good to me.''

Following Nick back into the living room, Caroline saw that before leaving, the bellboy had turned on the lamps and built a fire in the hearth, which now blazed cheerfully, somehow giving the cabin the ambience of a lover's retreat. As a result, she couldn't seem to stop dwelling on the single bedroom.

What had her grandmother been thinking of? It wasn't like Kate not to handle any matter competently—and Caroline just couldn't imagine that under the circumstances, her grandmother would deliberately have instructed the lodge to book the honeymoon cabin. So either the lodge itself had made the error—or Kate was finally slipping into senility.

Caroline couldn't believe this last. She didn't *want* to believe it. The idea that her grandmother wouldn't go on forever—omnipresent, intelligent and energetic—both frightened and dismayed her. No, the lodge had made a mistake, that was all.

"Why don't you unpack first, Nick, while I put the groceries away," Caroline suggested as she moved into the kitchen and switched on the soffit lights. They were fluorescent and flickered erratically for a moment before coming on, dispelling the loverlike atmosphere of the cabin, to her relief.

She began to take the groceries from the brown paper sacks sitting on the counter. On their way here, Nick had instructed the limousine driver to stop at one of the local markets. There, Caroline had loaded a cart with enough food to last the week, her grandmother having warned them that since the lodge's dining room closed early and there was no twenty-four hour room service, they would be wise to have a few essentials on hand, especially if they wanted to do any cooking of their own.

"Each cabin comes equipped with a fully stocked kitchen," Kate had explained. "So you'll have everything you might need in the way of pots and pans and other utensils."

Now, as Caroline opened the cabinets, she saw that this was indeed true. "How about if I fix a couple of these steaks tonight, Nick?" She held up a package wrapped in butcher's paper.

"How about if we grill them together?" he replied, smiling at her. "After all, it's our wedding night, so it doesn't seem fair that just one of us should do the cooking."

"I suppose we *could* order something in from the lodge," she said tentatively.

"What? And make some poor fellow have to lug a heavy tray out here in the dark and in this weather? No, that's too mean even to contemplate, baby," Nick insisted. "He's liable to slip on the icy ground, slide down into some overgrown ravine and be eaten by wolves or a bear attracted by our nuptial dinner. And probably, the poor guy's bones won't be found until spring. Besides, we're newlyweds, remember? And honeymooners value their privacy. We've got all we need right here—and anyway, it'll give us something to do."

Caroline flushed as his dark eyes raked her appraisingly and an insolent grin curved his mouth, so she received the unmistakable impression that *cooking* was really the last thing he wanted to be doing on his wedding night. It wasn't exactly how, over the years, she had envisioned spending this evening, either. But then, she had never dreamed of an arranged marriage in name only or anything else that had occurred these past few days. She still felt as though she were caught up in some wild dream, riding upon some crazy carousel. But would it prove to have a brass ring—and if it did, could she, *would* she, be able to grab it?

She didn't know.

To take her mind off the fact that she was totally alone with a very attractive, virile man who just happened to be her husband, Caroline concentrated on putting away the groceries. She was relieved when Nick disappeared into the bedroom to unpack. His effect upon her was nothing short of devastating. She didn't know how she was going to endure being alone here in this cabin with him for an entire week.

She would like to give the reservation clerk at the front desk a piece of her mind for making such an error about the cabin, she thought, annoyed, her nerves jumping.

Nick Valkov plus one bedroom. For a week.

She didn't need to be a chemist to figure out that that was undoubtedly an explosive equation.

Seven

Caroline unbagged the fresh spinach and the romaine, red and butter lettuces and started to tear off their leaves, filling the sink with cold water to rinse them. She would make a tossed salad to go with the steaks, she decided, and a couple of twice-baked potatoes and a vegetable. A medley of steamed broccoli, cauliflower and carrots would be good. Then she realized she didn't know if Nick liked any of those foods.

"I do," he announced moments later when she asked him. "Your turn to unpack. Tomatoes and purple onions in the salad?"

"You read my mind," Caroline called back lightly over her shoulder as she headed toward the bedroom.

There, she unlocked her two Louis Vuitton cases and began to put her clothes away. Nick, she saw, had left her more than half of the closet space and the entire armoire, taking the dresser for himself. That spoke well of him, she thought. It showed he was considerate and knew how to share. His own garments were hung and folded neatly, another mark in his favor.

Thank heavens he wasn't a slob! She couldn't have lived with that.

There was so much she didn't know about Nick, Caroline belatedly recognized. *Three days.* She had only known him, really, for three days. Even now, it was hard for her to believe she had actually married him this morning. But she had, she thought as she hung her own clothes in the closet and folded others to tuck them into the armoire. He wasn't anything at all like what she had previously imagined.

Now she realized how lucky she was that he was a decent man. But of course, her grandmother would never have suggested this marriage if she had believed Nick to be anything other than that, Caroline grasped slowly. In fact, now that she thought about it, she knew Kate must think extremely highly of Nick—and not just as a chemist, either, but also as a man. Because there was no way her grandmother would have married her off to just anyone, sent her away with him, alone, to an isolated place like the Maplewood Lodge for a week—not even to save the secret youth formula.

That realization lessened some of the anxiety Caroline had felt ever since discovering that the cabin had only one bedroom. She returned to the kitchen to find the steaks cooking on the grill and Nick tossing the salad. She pitched in by cutting up the vegetables and preparing the potatoes. From the ease with which she and Nick worked together in the kitchen, she thought that anyone observing them would believe they had been married for years instead of for less than a day.

"Do you want to be very formal and dine at the table?" he inquired as he expertly flipped the steaks. "Or would you rather eat casually on the coffee table, in front of the fireplace?"

"You mean like at a slumber party?" Caroline suggested—then could have bitten off her tongue. She blushed crimson with embarrassment at Nick's mocking grin.

"Well, if that's what you have in mind, baby..."

"It's not! And what's more, you know it!" To avoid his amused but smoldering gaze, she lifted the pot lid, pretending to check on the vegetables steaming on the stove.

"Ah. Do I, now? For all I know, it might have been a Freudian slip."

"It wasn't," Caroline insisted, still flushed, her heart thrumming so crazily that she felt as though it might leap from her breast. She thumped the lid back onto the pot. "It's just that I associate eating on a coffee table with girlish things like slumber parties. It's what my sisters and I used to do when we were in our teens...pop corn, lounge around the fireplace, tell spooky stories. You know? Like the one about the mysterious girl at the high school prom who turns out to have been killed in a car accident on prom night years before, or the lovers parked in the woods and the escaped convict with a steel hook for a hand, who creeps up on them. . . ." Her voice trailed away as she watched Nick's shoulders begin to shake with merriment before he actually burst out laughing, a deep, rich sound.

"This is what American teenage girls do for fun at slumber parties?" he asked.

"Well, yes, among other things," Caroline confirmed reluctantly, abashed.

"Such as?"

"Such as sticking the hands of the girls who fall asleep in bowls of ice water and freezing their underwear— Oh, God! It all sounds so terribly silly, doesn't it? I can't believe I actually used to do things like that."

"Neither can I," Nick declared, still grinning. "Perhaps it's just as well that I will be relegated to an uncomfortable night on one of the love seats. Because I certainly don't want to awaken in the morning and find my boxer shorts as stiff as a board. Why, Caro, have I said something amiss? You're blushing again. I meant only that you might be tempted to stick them into the freezer, should I be so foolish as to fall asleep. . . ."

From the way his dark eyes danced wickedly, she knew that was *not* what he had meant. And it was certainly *not* the image his words had conjured up in her mind, but a sexy picture of Nick naked save for his underwear—and highly aroused. Unwittingly, she speculated about his boxer shorts, whether they were silk....

Good God, what was the matter with her? Caroline wondered, bewildered—and somehow excited despite herself. She didn't normally dwell on thoughts of sex or engage in risqué conversation with a man. And *this* man was her husband. Why, he might take her behavior as an invitation to crawl into her bed later!

Why in the hell did he have to be so damnably male and attractive, anyway?

Chemists were supposed to be dull, boring fuddy-duddies or wild, eccentric fruitcakes, weren't they? Puttering around in dusty, cluttered old laboratories, amid piles of moldering books and a jumbled array of boiling beakers. They didn't wear Armani suits and smoke Player's cigarettes and drink Stolichnaya vodka. They didn't grill steaks and make licentious remarks and set anything besides a Bunsen burner aflame—certainly not a cool, sophisticated woman such as herself!

That dumb, smirking bellboy had just turned the cabin's thermostat up way too high—and combined with the heat from the oven, the stove and the fireplace, it was simply too much, that was all. Why, it was practically roasting in the cabin, Caroline thought. She should take off the sweater she had tossed on over her blouse earlier. No, she couldn't do that. Nick might deliberately misconstrue that action, too.

"Perhaps we'd better eat at the table," she said, flustered.

"We can watch television in the living room," Nick reminded her. "Catch the news."

"Yes, all right, fine." At least that way, she wouldn't have to tax her brain, trying to carry on an innocuous dialogue with him.

She busied herself with taking the potatoes from the oven and dishing up the vegetables from the stove, while he lifted the steaks from the grill, putting one on each plate. A few minutes later, he and she were seated on the floor before the coffee table, the television tuned to CNN. But to Caroline's dismay, the news didn't deter Nick from conversation, after all.

"Champagne for the bride and groom." He filled their crystal flutes half full from the bottle of Krug he had opened earlier. Then he lifted his glass. "I can think of a great many Russian wedding toasts. Unfortunately, my English fails me at the moment. So... to us, Caro," he said softly.

"To us," she echoed, touching her flute lightly to his own.

They sipped the champagne, Caroline drinking far more than she knew she ought. Beyond a few glass-fuls of wine, she had no head for alcohol, and too much champagne always wreaked havoc on her senses. The bubbles tickled her nose: the wine itself seemed to rush through her body, giddying her.

Even now, she stubbornly didn't want to admit to herself that it was Nick and not the champagne who was having such a strange, dazing effect upon her.

She had best get some food in her stomach before she wound up drunk and not responsible for her actions, Caroline thought, turning her attention to her plate.

"Is your steak all right? You did say medium rare, didn't you?" Nick asked.

"Yes, it's great . . . but much more than I'll be able to eat, I know." She eyed the big, thick porterhouse a trifle ruefully. "We should have just split one, I suppose."

"Speak for yourself, baby. You know what they say. Man does not live by bread alone—and I intend to consume every bite of *my* steak." With relish, he attacked his own plate.

Until this moment, Caroline had not thought of the act of dining as an especially erotic experience. But even the way Nick ate was somehow seductive. His teeth were very straight and white against his bronzed skin. They sank into the tender steak in a fashion that made her think, involuntarily, of them sinking into her soft shoulder, taking little love bites down her nape and along the insides of her thighs. . . .

Heavens! She was doing it again, drifting off into a sensuous daydream about him, fantasizing about him! Cool, competent Caroline Fortune—imagining things that might have been scenes from an R-rated movie.

The champagne had definitely affected her for the worse. She would *not* drink any more of it!

Mortified, Caroline bent her head over her plate, hoping desperately that Nick couldn't read her thoughts. They simply *had* to be born of the fact that this was her wedding night—which she had never envisioned spending alone in her bed, especially with a tall, dark, handsome husband in the next room.

So near. And yet so far.

Eight

"Do you want dessert now or later, baby?" Nick inquired once he and Caroline had finished supper. Earlier, at the grocery store's bakery counter, he had spied a small, simple wedding cake topped by a bride and groom and had insisted on buying it.

"Later." She groaned, rubbing her stomach ruefully. "I don't think I could possibly manage another single bite at the moment. I don't remember the last time I ate so much."

"How about if I put some coffee on, then?"

"That sounds wonderful."

She helped him clean up and load the dishwasher. Then he started the coffeemaker, and when it was finished, they took their brimming cups into the living room, to sit again before the fire. Nick threw more logs onto the blaze, arranging them with the cast-iron poker.

"So. What shall we do now to entertain ourselves?" he asked, turning to smile at her slowly. "Tell each other spooky stories? I don't know any about long-dead debutantes and escaped convicts with hooks for hands, but I could probably manage a couple about Russian witches.''

''Thanks, but no thanks. I'm afraid I scare just as easily now as I did back during the days of my and my sisters' slumber parties. I'll only wind up lying in bed later and imagining you out here turning into a werewolf or something.''

''So that's how you see me, is it? As wolfish?'' Nick quirked one thick, dark eyebrow devilishly.

''Well . . . maybe a little,'' Caroline confessed.

''Relax, baby. Although I'll admit that the idea *is* tempting, I'm not going to gobble you up. You're safe with me.''

Much to her surprise, Caroline felt a strange sense of pique and disappointment at his words, as though she actually *did* want to be gobbled up by him. And that was ridiculous.

''How about a game of cards?'' she proposed, to divert herself—and him.

''You mean like . . . strip poker?'' He grinned roguishly.

''No, I do *not* mean like strip poker!'' She flushed, biting her lower lip. ''Honestly, Nick! Do you realize that every discussion we have seems to lead to—to . . . well, you know. To—to—''

''Sexual innuendos?'' he suggested, feigning helpfulness.

''Well . . . yes.''

"Caro, you're my wife—and this is our wedding night. And I'd be lying if I said that it hasn't crossed my mind to take you into that bedroom and make love to you. I'm a man, for heaven's sake. And you're a beautiful, alluring woman. I'm attracted to you—and I think perhaps you're attracted to me, too."

"How can you say that? You're—you're almost a stranger to me." She glanced down at her coffee cup, unable to go on meeting his eyes, afraid her own would somehow reveal to him just *how* attracted to him she was. She didn't want to make a fool of herself by succumbing to a man who had married her only to prevent himself from being deported. "I—I hardly know you."

"As any good chemist—and I am definitely one of those—could tell you, despite all the laws of science, there's still no accounting for the chemistry between a man and a woman. If it's there, it's there—regardless. If it's not, it's just not. And whether or not you know somebody has nothing whatsoever to do with it. It's a physical reaction—something that's all in the pheromones."

"So you don't think the mind or the emotions play any part in it whatsoever?" Caroline queried, curious and feeling somehow depressed by his words. Until this moment, she had begun to think she had previously misjudged Nick. Now she wondered if these past few days he had simply been on his best behavior, concealing his Old World tendencies toward women.

Because what he was talking about was sex, not love—and she had simply never been able to separate the two.

"No," he answered her question. "Attraction is all physical."

"Well, I suppose I should feel flattered. But it…just doesn't work that way for me, Nick. Before I become involved with a man, I like to think I know him, that we have many things in common, that we have… feelings for each other, that we *care* about each other. It just wouldn't seem right to me, otherwise."

"No, I imagine not. You're a romantic, Caro."

"And what's wrong with that?"

"Nothing—except that it frequently makes life a great deal more complicated."

"Why? Because you have to share yourself with another human being?"

"That's a part of it, yes," he rejoined slowly, staring down at his coffee cup, idly swirling its contents.

"And you don't like to do that?"

"I didn't say that, Caro."

"Not in so many words, perhaps. But it *is* what you meant, isn't it, Nick?"

"No, it isn't. What I meant was that for me to want to do that, I have to feel that the woman is special, that she's someone I could fall in love with. I believe that's true for most men, actually. We're not as inclined as women, I don't think, to examine our emotions too deeply unless we have cause to. So... how about that game of cards?'' He deftly changed the subject.

''We *are* talking about something like gin rummy, aren't we?'' Caroline asked, at once relieved and yet somehow oddly disappointed to be again on safer ground.

''If that's your pleasure. But just to make it a little more interesting, what do you say to the loser having to fix breakfast?''

''I say that's a deal.''

In the end, Caroline found not only a deck of cards, but also a cribbage board in the huge old cupboard that stood against one wall. So she and Nick played that, and despite the fact that she had always considered herself a very good cribbage player, she lost, her peg several holes behind his at the completion of the game.

''My luck was really out tonight, I guess,'' she commented ruefully as she gathered up the cards and cribbage board to put them away.

''Well, you know what they say. Lucky at cards, unlucky at love. So perhaps it works the other way, as well.''

''Maybe,'' she agreed lightly, getting to her feet. ''But somehow, I have the distinct impression that I'm not going to be asked out on too many dates when prospective suitors learn that I've already got a husband at home.''

Nick, in the process of taking their coffee cups into the kitchen, abruptly froze at that. Then, after a moment, he set the cups down and joined her at the cupboard just as she finished closing the drawer. "Caro, I am *so* sorry," he said quietly, taking her in his arms. "I don't know how I could have been so selfish, so stupid. But because I wasn't seeing anyone special and with everything that's happened and how fast, I just never even gave a thought to that aspect of the situation. God! I didn't even think to ask if you were seeing anyone. I just assumed—"

"No, it's all right. I wasn't, actually... dating anybody, I mean."

"Good. That's good, then, that I didn't mess anything up for you. But look, Caro, if you should want to—go out with anyone, that is—anytime during our marriage, I want you to know I... well, that I won't insist on fidelity. I'll...ah...turn a blind eye, as they say." But even as he spoke these words, Nick thought suddenly, fiercely, that he damned well *wouldn't* look the other way, that she was *his wife,* and that he didn't want her becoming involved with any man but him! Not just his possessiveness toward her, but also the ferocity of it startled him.

"Oh, Nick, I...don't know what to say—except that I—I couldn't do anything like that. I just wouldn't feel right about it. I know our marriage is one of convenience, but still, there might be...talk,

rumors flying around Fortune Cosmetics. Grandmother, for one, would just absolutely hit the roof!''

So would I, Nick thought grimly, although he didn't
speak the words aloud. Instead, he said, ''Of course
she would. She told me as much herself. Oh, not
meaning you, but me—that she expected me to do
right by you, to be a faithful husband. I have to admit I was a little insulted, because naturally, I hadn't
planned on being anything else. Nor will I be. So.
Shall we have that cake and some more coffee now?''

''Yes—and then I suppose we should flip a quarter
or something to decide who gets the bathroom first.''
With her hand, Caroline smothered a yawn. ''Forgive
me. But in case you haven't noticed, Nick, it *is* getting late—and I'm afraid my internal rhythms aren't
programmed for keeping me awake much past eleven,
especially after a couple of glasses of champagne.''

He laughed. ''Neither are mine, actually. That's
what comes of punching an early clock in the corporate world, I guess.''

They ate their cake, after which Caroline won the
coin toss. So while Nick rinsed their plates, she ran the
water for her bath, pouring in a fragranced oil man-
ufactured by Fortune Cosmetics for just this purpose. Then, after making sure she had towels and her
negligee and robe, she locked the bathroom door behind her and took off her clothes. She felt strange and
not a little uncomfortable performing such intimate,
personal tasks with Nick in the next room. But then

she reminded herself that no matter what, he *was* her husband and she was going to be living with him like this from now on—or at least until he was safe from the INS and the two of them could obtain a quiet divorce.

Caroline slipped into the bathwater, telling herself that regardless of how she might wish to linger, that wasn't a good idea. After the champagne she had drunk, she might accidentally fall asleep in the bathtub—and then Nick might wind up having to break down the door to prevent her from drowning. She imagined him lifting her naked body in his arms, carrying her into the bedroom, laying her down upon the bed, compelled to give her artificial respiration. Except that in her mind, his mouth-to-mouth efforts to save her turned into passionate kisses....

With a start, Caroline jerked awake, realizing abruptly that she actually *had* nodded off. She forced herself to sit upright in the bathtub, to splash water repeatedly on her face until she was certain she wouldn't fall asleep again.

"Caro. *Caro!*" Nick rapped sharply, peremptorily, on the bathroom door, then rattled the knob vigorously. "Are you all right in there?"

"Yes. *Yes!*" she called frantically, anxiously clutching the washcloth to her breasts, apprehensive that at any moment her imaginings were about to become a reality, that he would kick down the door.

"Well, what's taking you so long, then? I got worried about you."

"I'm sorry. I . . . ah . . . was daydreaming, I guess," she explained lamely, for there was no way she was going to tell him she had nodded off. He might think she was still dozing, talking in her sleep, and come crashing through the door.

That fear spurring her on, she scrambled from the bathtub, hastily drying herself off and yanking on her negligee and robe. She brushed her teeth quickly, debating about whether or not to wash off her makeup. It wasn't good to leave it on overnight; her grandmother had warned her so a thousand times. But there was no way, Caroline decided, that she was going to let Nick see her without it—at least, not just yet.

"Like you should care, Caro," she muttered to herself. "You'd better get a handle on this situation, keep reminding yourself that this is a marriage in name only!"

She unlocked the bathroom door—not expecting to find herself face-to-face with Nick. When she did, she jumped, startled, her hand flying to her mouth to stifle her gasp.

"Oh." Caroline laughed weakly. "You scared me, Nick."

"I didn't mean to. Are you sure you're all right?" His brow was knitted with concern as he gazed down at her.

"Of course. Why wouldn't I be?"

"Well, I don't know, Caro—except that you told me you were tired, and then you went into that damned bathroom and stayed there for nearly an hour."

"An hour! I—I didn't realize." She must have been asleep for far longer than just a few moments, Caroline thought, dismayed. It was a wonder she *hadn't* drowned! "I'm sorry. It really *has* been a long day, Nick."

"Yeah, I know. So why don't you go on to bed? I'll grab my shower, try to make as little noise as possible." Nick didn't add that if she didn't get into bed and out of the light, he was going to have to take a very *cold* shower. But he recognized that something of this must have shown upon his face, because suddenly, Caroline nodded, swallowing hard and clutching the edges of her robe together as she pushed past him wordlessly, doing her best not to brush against him.

Nick swore softly in Russian and disappeared into the bathroom, nearly slamming the door behind him. Damn! Celibacy was going to be a lot harder than he had thought. Why in the hell had he ever agreed to this crazy marriage? He should have just let the INS deport him!

The water from the shower head hit him in an icy blast, taking his breath away, driving like needles into his skin. He couldn't stand it. Whoever had suggested this as a cure for what ailed him was a complete sadist! he thought. Shivering, Nick turned on the hot tap, groaning when he remembered the sight of Car-

oline's soft, negligee-clothed body illuminated by the
light from the bathroom and bedroom. He had been
able to see the sweet curve of her breasts—too full,
really, for her to have been a technically perfect
model—and a hint of her dusky nipples, the arch of
her slender hips, the length of her racy legs.

He had wanted to grab her up and fling her down
upon the bed, rip off her negligee and make love to her
until the wee hours. Unbidden into his mind had come
the thought that he was bigger and stronger than she
and that he *was* her husband—to say nothing of the
fact that she probably wouldn't tell anyone if he didn't
keep his part of the bargain in their arranged marriage. He had been so tempted.

But he wasn't Paul Andersen, and Nick couldn't
and wouldn't hurt Caroline that way. Even if she had
responded to him, she would have been humiliated and
ashamed afterward. As a result, she might even have
been driven to file for a divorce—and then her grandmother would surely have demanded to know why.

Nick didn't scare at all easily. Still, Kate Winfield
Fortune on a tear wasn't someone he particularly
wanted to tangle with.

No, as the saying went, he would just have to grin
and bear it. He groaned again at the thought. Step-
ping from the shower, he toweled himself dry, then
pulled on the pajama bottoms and robe he had packed
out of deference to Caroline's sensibilities.

Opening the bathroom door, he saw that she had left the lamp burning on the night table, so he wouldn't have to make his way in the dark to the living room.

"Caro, are you asleep?" he asked quietly as he moved toward the brass bed.

"Hmmm. Almost," she murmured drowsily, stretching and yawning.

Like a kitten, he thought, his groin tightening with desire. In truth, she wasn't really awake. He could slip in beside her, take her in his arms and consummate their marriage before she even knew what was happening....

No, he couldn't do that, damn it!

"Caro... Good night, baby. Happy wedding day," he whispered, then bent and kissed her lightly on the mouth before shutting off the lamp and reluctantly tiptoeing from the bedroom.

In the living room, he saw that Caroline had thoughtfully done her best to make up one of the love seats for him, with a pillow and blankets. He settled his six-feet-one inches into the makeshift bed as best as he was able, groaning and silently cursing whatever fool had screwed up the reservation so that he and Caroline had wound up in the honeymoon cabin instead of one with two bedrooms.

As he drifted into slumber, Nick thought that if he ever discovered the identity of the person responsible, he would wring the idiot's damned neck!

Nine

As Kate Fortune gazed out the wide bank of windows in her penthouse office at Fortune Cosmetics, she couldn't repress a delighted giggle. She would have given anything to have seen the expressions on Caroline's and Nick's faces when they had realized they had been installed in the honeymoon cabin at Maplewood Lodge.

Of course, Kate hadn't been able to direct her secretary, Louise Rhymer, to make such a reservation—or even to make it herself, for that matter. Although she had known both Louise and Will Bentley, the proprietor of Maplewood Lodge, for years and trusted their discretion, still, it was possible that they would inadvertently let something slip to someone and then the newlyweds might have learned what Kate had done.

Even so, she had managed the affair easily enough. She had instructed her housekeeper to make the arrangements—knowing that if anything ever got out, she could blame the mix-up on Mrs. Brant.

Now, as Kate glanced at the dreary gray winter sky, she wondered if it was snowing across the border in

Canada, at the Maplewood Lodge. She certainly hoped so, hoped that Caroline and Nick were stuck in their one-bedroom cabin, alone with each other—and doing what came naturally between a handsome man and a beautiful woman in such a situation.

Their marriage was simply *not* going to end in an annulment or a divorce—not if she could help it!

Already, rumors about Caroline and Nick having eloped were circulating through Fortune Cosmetics. And although Kate had not confirmed any of the gossip, she had not denied it, either, merely smiled mysteriously at the polite, carefully phrased questions, so that it would become generally known throughout the company that if such an event *had* occurred, she would not be disapproving. She had instructed Jake and Sterling to take the same tack.

Passing Paul Andersen in one of the long corridors earlier in the day, Kate had nodded and positively beamed at him, knowing from the expression on his face that he had heard the news about Caroline and Nick and was dying to be told it wasn't true.

Not a chance, Paul, you idiot, Kate had thought smugly to herself as she had strolled briskly by him. *You're lucky you even still have a job here at Fortune Cosmetics after breaking my granddaughter's heart!*

Surreptitiously peeking back over her shoulder, Kate had taken a great deal of satisfaction in seeing Paul stick a finger under his collar and run it back and forth, as though his tie were choking him. Over the years, she had learned how, with a glance cast just so, to do that to people who had displeased her, making them wonder nervously if she was about to fire them. On more than one occasion, she had done so, because she would not tolerate any employee who couldn't cut the mustard at Fortune Cosmetics. Those who excelled at their jobs were equally as quick to be rewarded.

Be tough but fair, her late husband, Ben, had always been fond of saying, and Kate had adopted that motto for her own.

Now, turning from the windows, Kate abruptly strode purposefully from her office. She could have just called down to the laboratory. But she knew she would get nothing over the telephone from the stolid Otto Mueller. Face-to-face, however, he would not find it so easy to fob her off in Nick's absence. And even though only a few days had passed since Nick's formal presentation about her secret youth formula, she just *had* to know how Fabulous Face was progressing, whether or not they were any closer to discovering the identity of Ingredient X.

"Good morning, Otto." Kate greeted the heavyset chemist pleasantly and smiled warmly as she entered the laboratory, causing him inwardly to groan.

Like everyone else at Fortune Cosmetics, Otto knew that when his employer chirruped as brightly and charmingly as a bird, it was wise to be on guard. In response, he grunted taciturnly before pointedly turning his attention once more to his work.

"Otto, I want to know if we've eliminated any more possibilities for Ingredient X within the last few days." Kate was undeterred by his terseness.

"Yes." He nodded, volunteering no further information.

"Oh, for pity's sake, Otto! Your loyalty and discretion are admirable. But how many times do I have to remind you that you work for me—and not Nick Valkov! Now, I want to know about Ingredient X!"

"Amazon," the chemist finally said reluctantly.

"Amazon? Well, what in the hell is that supposed to mean? Explain yourself. I swear, getting more than a word or two out of you is like pulling teeth. Are you referring to the Amazon jungle?"

"Yes." Otto sighed heavily, knowing he was going to have to talk to her, whether he wanted to or not. Then Nick would be mad when he returned to the laboratory, because he didn't like anyone—not even Kate—meddling in his domain. And then Otto would like as not find himself on the receiving end of another one of Nick's pranks. "I think that's where Ingredient X is going to be found. But I can't say for sure, you understand. I still have more tests to run."

"How many tests?"

"I don't know. But several. As Nick and I both have pointed out to you many times before, science cannot be rushed, Mrs. Fortune. You don't want us to make a mistake in here, do you? Accidentally turn your Fabulous Face into Frightening Face?''

''No, of course not.''

''Then you simply must be patient,'' the chemist insisted stubbornly.

''Well, still, what are we talking about here, Otto? Days? Weeks? Months?''

''Weeks, maybe—*if* you're lucky. And *if* you leave me in peace to get on with my work!'' Otto glowered at her, indicating the beakers and test tubes, the microscope and slides, and the ream of notes arrayed before him.

Scowling back and tapping her foot impatiently, Kate debated pressing him further. But she knew from the mulish set of his jaw that she would likely get nothing more from him—the obstinate old goat! If he weren't so brilliant, she would send him packing, she fumed.

It never occurred to Kate that in all the departments at Fortune Cosmetics, she had people in charge who shared many of her own traits, that she actually secretly enjoyed these little skirmishes with Otto and various other of her employees. They kept her sharp, on her toes.

More than once, she had been tempted to play some trick on Otto, in order to disconcert him, he was so impossibly down to earth. Nevertheless, she had steadfastly resisted the impulse, deeming it undignified for a woman in her position. She knew Nick, however, was not so restrained, and she chuckled whenever she happened to hear the latest joke he had pulled on his fellow chemist.

Last time, Nick had poured some harmless chemical into the laboratory's coffeepot. Otto had gone around half the day with a discolored mouth and tongue. Agnes Grimsby, who ran the company's cafeteria and was sweet on the chemist, had nearly fainted when she had seen him at lunch—especially when Nick had slyly suggested that Agnes's cooking was to blame for the mishap.

"All right, Otto. I can take a hint," Kate declared tartly. "Go on back to your tests. But mind you notify me the moment you've made any further progress."

Already, Kate was mulling over the germ of an idea with regard to Ingredient X. The secret youth formula was *her* baby. She had dreamed of it for years— and now that it was finally nearing completion, she ought to be the one who provided the last piece of the equation.

Once she knew what that was, she would fly down to the Amazon, piloting the corporate jet herself, Kate decided. She couldn't tell anyone, not even Sterling, of her plan, however. All her family and friends would be violently opposed to the scheme. They would point out what a long, tiring trip it was, how she was too elderly to undertake such a strenuous journey, especially at the plane's controls herself. But Kate knew that thanks to a regular regime of exercise, she was fitter than a lot of women decades younger than she.

Yes, she would go to the Amazon jungle herself.

Amelia Earhart had nothing on Kate Fortune!

Ten

To Caroline and Nick, the week at Maplewood Lodge seemed to pass all too quickly, despite the fact that the pace of life in the cabin was actually slow. The winter continued to be abysmally cold, the sky sullen and misty, the days gray and dreary. More than once, the newlyweds awakened to fresh snowfall that draped the swells and hollows of the earth like a pristine blanket. The boughs of the trees wept teardrops in the form of icicles, and a hard layer of rime encrusted the ground.

Still, the weather did not deter Caroline and Nick from going outside. They took sleigh rides accompanied by the musical jingle of the bells on the horses' harnesses, and long walks in the woods, fogging the air with their breath. They built a big snow bride and groom in the front yard of the cabin, and from behind walls of snow heaped high, they conducted vigorous battles with snowballs, which ended in them rolling on the ground, laughing, sodden and breathless.

Inside, they would take turns in the bathroom, stripping off their wet clothes, then bundling up in clean, warm garments, after which they would curl up before the cheerfully blazing fireplace, cups of hot chocolate in hand. They played cards and board games from the stock in the antique cupboard and music on the stereo. CNN kept them apprised of the news, and they talked endlessly.

Caroline had never before lived with a man. In fact, she had not lived with anyone since she had moved away from home during her college years to make her own way in the world. She had not realized until now how very alone she had been, how much she had missed the company of another human being. It was pleasant to have someone to share the household chores with, to carry on a conversation with, to take pride in her accomplishments.

"Caro baby!" Nick called more than once. "Hurry! Your commercial's on!"

Each time, she ran dutifully into the living room, where her sister Allie's face would smile back at her from the television screen and the voice-over would promote Fortune Cosmetics' foundation or mascara, lipstick or nail polish. Despite that Caroline had viewed the advertisements umpteen times, that she had, in fact, been responsible for the original concept, she still never tired of seeing them, and was secretly thrilled by this physical evidence of her success.

"I remember developing that color... Cinnamon Stick," Nick observed as, on the television screen,

Allie puckered up her lips to blow a playful kiss at the handsome, admiring man in the scene.

"It's one of our most popular shades of lipstick and nail polish," Caroline said, feeling warm clear down to her toes at the idea that Nick was proud of her work, that it was her he thought of when he saw the commercials—not Allie, not Kate—but her, Caroline.

"Hmmm. Is that so?" Nick lifted one thick, dark brow. "Well, I've got a notion brewing for a new color when we get back to work—and I bet it will wind up outselling all the others. In fact, I've already got a name for it."

"Oh?" she replied archly, sauntering toward him. "Since when do chemists name products at Fortune Cosmetics? And just what were you thinking of calling it, anyway?"

"Caroline's Kiss. I've got something in mind that's sweet and spicy and sensual all at the same time." Reaching out from where he lounged upon the floor, Nick grabbed Caroline's ankle, pulling her foot from beneath her so she toppled into his lap. Rolling her over, he pressed her down upon the rug. "And I don't expect to have any arguments with the marketing department about it."

"Uh-huh. Well, don't think that just because you're married to the vice president, you're going to receive any special privileges at the company—because you're not," Caroline insisted, her heart hammering at the feel of his hard, lean, muscular body lying atop her soft, slender, one. His lips were just inches from her own. His eyes danced and smoldered like the embers that flew from the fire blazing in the hearth.

"Oh, I'm not, am I? Well, we'll just have to see about that, won't we?" Nick muttered huskily before his mouth claimed hers, his tongue insidiously parting her lips and shooting deep between them, seeking and savoring.

Involuntarily, Caroline moaned and opened her mouth pliantly to his. Of their own accord, her arms slipped up to twine around his neck. Her fingers burrowed through his thick, dark hair. Inside her, desire awakened and burgeoned. No matter how hard she had tried to fight her attraction to Nick, it seemed he had only to touch her like this and she softened and melted like candle wax. Her body felt weak and boneless as his lips moved on hers, growing fiercer, more insistent. His tongue followed the contours of her mouth. His teeth nibbled her lower lip, causing an electric tingle to radiate through her.

Caroline knew she ought not let him kiss her like this. It would only lead to trouble in the end, she thought, disheartened. He had made it clear to her that he believed attraction was purely physical, relied solely on chemistry, on pheromones—and had nothing whatsoever to do with the mind or emotions at all. And she just couldn't think that way. Like it or not, she knew that despite herself, Nick stirred more than just a biological response in her. This past week, she had begun to have feelings toward him.

More than once, she had totally forgotten that theirs was a marriage of convenience, that her grandmother and father had as much as hired Nick to wed her, so the secret youth formula would be saved. She mustn't keep forgetting that, Caroline had told herself on each of those occasions—just as she did now. But emotions just weren't something she could turn on and off like a faucet, especially when she was lying in his arms like this and he was making her feel womanly and desirable. Still, she didn't want to be used and hurt, to have her heart broken again.

"Nick...Nick..." she murmured as his mouth slanted hotly across her cheek to her temple. "You— you mustn't do this. *We* mustn't do it."

"Why not?" He nipped her earlobe gently, his breath warm against her skin, sending a shiver through her. "You're my wife, Caro. I'm your husband."

"I—I know...but in name only, remember? And I just can't put that fact aside and forget it simply because you want me to at the moment, Nick. Once your troubles with the INS are over, *we'll* be over. You know that," she reminded him quietly.

"Yeah, I guess you're right." Reluctantly, sighing heavily, he rolled off her, helping her sit up. Inwardly, he groaned as his gaze took in her mussed hair, her flushed cheeks, the pulse that beat erratically at the delicate hollow of her slender throat. Keeping his hands off her was proving increasingly difficult. The more time he spent with her, the more he wanted her. "I'm sorry, Caro. I don't have any excuse—except that a man would have to be dead not to desire you, and I'm very much alive." *And in my prime and not accustomed to living like a monk, either,* he added mentally, although he didn't speak the words aloud.

Caroline laughed tremulously. "I guess I should be flattered, actually. Look, Nick, it's late, so I think I'll go ahead and take a bath, then turn in."

"Yeah, all right, fine. I'll...ah...just read for a while, listen to some music until you're done. I don't get much rest on that love seat, anyway."

She flushed at that, upset. "You know I've offered several times to let you have the bed. It just doesn't make sense for you to sleep out here when I'm smaller and would do just fine on the love seat."

"No." He shook his head. "My 'Old World tendencies,' as you call them, are not so marked that they include forcing my wife to sleep on a couch. Besides, what's one more night, anyway?"

The reminder that they were going home tomorrow depressed Caroline no end. For the first time that she could remember, she wasn't anxious, eager, to return to work. She wished she and Nick had been able to take more than a week off for their honeymoon, that they could have stayed here at Maplewood Lodge for a month or more. But that wasn't possible. The secret youth formula was too important to Kate for her to tolerate their absence any longer than that—even if she *had* arranged their honeymoon in the first place.

Sighing as heavily as Nick had just moments ago, Caroline rose and headed for the bathroom. A short while later, she slipped into bed, feeling strangely as though she were on the verge of tears. She hadn't been as happy in a long time as she had this week. She should have let Nick make love to her, she reflected as she struggled beneath the covers. It was silly to kid herself that she had done the right thing in stopping him—because her heart said otherwise.

As she drifted toward sleep, unbidden into her mind came the thought, the *fear,* that she was foolishly falling in love with her hired husband.

Eleven

Caroline awoke abruptly, her teeth chattering. Despite the covers under which she huddled, she was freezing. The bedroom felt as though it were thirty degrees below zero. Turning on the lamp, she could see that her breath made white clouds in the air.

"Ni—Ni—Nick," she called, shivering violently and chafing her arms in an effort to warm them.

"Here I am. Hang on, baby." He strode through the doorway, carrying an armful of logs, which he dumped on the fieldstone fireplace in the bedroom before beginning to stack them in the hearth.

"Wh—wh—what's happened?" Caroline asked.

"The heat's gone off in the cabin. I phoned the front desk, but it seems there're no maintenance personnel on duty after midnight, so there's nobody to fix the furnace until tomorrow morning. We'll have to warm up the old-fashioned way. No, don't get out of bed, Caro! For heaven's sake, do you want to catch your death of cold? Get back under those blankets. There's nothing you can do to help me. I'll handle it."

She would have been lying to herself if she had not admitted she was relieved not to have to leave what little heat the bed provided. This was one of the advantages of having a husband with Old World tendencies, she guessed. He expected to take care of her in a situation such as this.

Nick built the fire and ignited the tinder and kindling. Then he disappeared into the kitchen, only to return shortly afterward with a steaming cup of what she initially supposed was hot chocolate.

"No, it's a hot toddy, actually," Nick announced. "Tea laced with brandy. The best thing in the world to warm you up quickly. Also good for colds—and for preventing them. I don't want you to get sick, so drink up, Caro."

While she gulped the toddy, grateful for its warmth, he took up the poker to stoke the fire, then added another log, so the blaze was soon burning nicely, beginning to dispel the chilliness of the bedroom. After that, before Caroline realized what he intended, Nick shrugged off his robe and climbed into bed with her.

"What do you think you're doing, Nick?" she cried softly.

"Sharing body heat. Here, are you finished with that?" He took the empty cup from her hands. "Good girl. Snuggle up, now." Burrowing beneath the blankets, he gathered her into his embrace, then reached over and flicked off the lamp, so only the glow of the crackling fire illuminated the bedroom, casting dancing shadows on the walls.

Despite the anxiety and strange anticipation she felt at lying with Nick in the same bed, Caroline had to admit that at least she was now warming up. Unlike hers, his body was like a furnace, generating heat. The brandy in the tea had helped her tremendously, too. Cradled against Nick's broad, furry chest, his strong arms wrapped securely and comfortingly around her, she felt pleasantly safe and drowsy, no longer cold.

"Better?" he asked softly.

"Yes, much."

"Good, I'm glad."

Later, Caroline blamed the brandy, even though in her heart of hearts, she knew nothing and no one but herself was responsible for not uttering a single word of protest when, after a time, Nick began gently to kiss and caress her. She understood what motivated him, because far from drifting back to sleep as she had grown warmer, she had instead become increasingly aware of him beside her, holding her. Of the feel of his bare chest beneath her cheek and the palm of her hand. Of the steady, reassuring beat of his heart against her ear. Of the strength of his body corded by powerful muscles. Of the fact that he was awake—and aroused.

However their marriage had come about, Nick *was* her husband, and no matter what, she *did* want him, Caroline thought. It was the chemistry they had talked about, pure and simple. How much longer could she go on fighting her feelings for him? A day? A week?

A month? If she were honest with herself, she knew that in the end, she would undoubtedly weaken and give in to temptation. This past week had shown her how difficult it was going to be to live with him—and not succumb. So why not surrender now and get it over with? Then maybe she could get him out of her system. The fact that she might only want him more, might lose her heart wholly to him, she determinedly shoved from her thoughts.

It was the brandy, she told herself, that had muddled her mind and confused her thinking so. But deep down inside, Caroline knew that was not true as she yielded to the onslaught of Nick's seductive mouth.

His tongue parted her lips, thrusting into the warm, moist cavern of her mouth. His hands tangled in her hair as he half turned his body, so she was shifted on to her back, his leg riding between her thighs. The silken folds of her negligee rubbed sensuously against her legs as his body moved against hers, one hand sweeping down to stroke her breasts, her belly, her soft mound, flitting here and there like a butterfly, lingering nowhere, lightly touching, taunting, arousing her wildly and leaving her aching for more.

Caroline whimpered against Nick's mouth as he continued to kiss and caress her, and the sound seemed to inflame him. He groaned and deepened his kisses, his body abruptly covering her own, his hands at the short, puffed sleeves of her negligee, roughly hauling them from her shoulders, sliding them down her arms until she was naked to the waist. Her breasts were soft and full, swollen with rising passion, their dusky crests taut beneath his slowly circling palms. His thumbs skimmed the flushed, engorged peaks.

His lips scorched her throat, seized one upthrusting nipple, imprisoning it. His tongue darted forth, licking, laving. Caroline arched against him, waves of delight and excitement rippling through her body. She clung to him, her fingers tunneling through his hair, digging into his shoulders as he continued to torment her, his breath hot and rasping against her naked flesh. Slowly, he drew his tongue up the valley between her breasts, captured her lips once more, his tongue delving deep, taking her breath. His mouth burned across her cheek to her temple, her ear. He bit her lobe gently.

"Caro," he muttered thickly. "You haven't said anything...not one word. Do you want me to stop? Because if you do, you had better tell me now. Otherwise, I warn you, I am likely to forget that I'm a gentleman and remember only that you're my wife. So...do you want me to continue or not?"

"Yes..." Was that really her voice, so soft, so breathless? Caroline wondered, shocked. She must be mad or drunk, she thought, to have told him to proceed. Still, she couldn't seem to call the word back, not even when, hearing it, he inhaled sharply, then swiftly but smoothly stripped off her negligee and panties, as though he feared she would change her mind. Then he divested himself of his boxer shorts—they *were* silk, Caroline noted dazedly, then averted her eyes, blushing as the evidence of his desire for her was revealed.

His physique was as magnificent as she had imagined, his belly a washboard of muscle, his sex hard and heavy. He drew her into his arms again, so their naked flesh met, and dimly, in some dark corner of her mind, she realized she wasn't cold at all anymore.

"Oh, baby." Nick sighed deeply with pleasure as his mouth and hands roamed over her body, igniting it much as he had the fire he had built earlier. "You don't know how badly I've wanted you. It's been hell for me all week, wondering how I was going to stand being married to you and not really having you as mine. Caro, you're sure this is what you want?"

"Yes," she whispered, trembling against him with the passion he had stirred in her.

"You're not going to regret it in the morning?"

"Probably, but it doesn't matter. Make love to me, Nick. Please."

"Yes, I will...all night, if you want. Spread your legs for me, sweetheart. Yes, like that. You're so beautiful, so soft...."

His hand found her, cupped her mound, rested there gently for a moment. At his touch, Caroline's breath caught in her throat, and then a low moan issued from her lips. Nick kissed her hungrily again, swallowing the sound, her breath. His tongue plunged into her mouth as his fingers slid deep inside her, only to withdraw, then push into her again. And again. And all the while, his thumb moved on the little bud concealed in the fragile petals of her, stroking, teasing, making her long to be filled by him.

Instinctively, Caroline writhed and strained against him, unable to think anymore, a mass of sensation, giddy, breathless. She clutched Nick to her, her palms slipping down his sweat-sheened back and buttocks, tracing the strong curve of muscles that bunched and quivered beneath her palms. Wordlessly, she tried to tell him of her need, bucked against his hand. But he ignored her silent plea, continuing to torment her. Lowering his head to her breast, he took her nipple between his lips, sucking greedily, while his hand continued to fondle her.

An unendurable pressure built steadily within her, higher and higher, until it was a flood that could no longer be contained and burst inside her, rushing through her in wave after wave of pleasure that left her gasping and crying out.

Only then did Nick poise himself above her, the powerful muscles in his arms flexing as he entered her, drove down into her, piercing her to the core. For a moment, he was still, his heart beating violently against Caroline's own, their uneven breathing mingling in the silence broken only by the cracking and sparking of a log on the fire. Smiling down at her, he kissed her mouth, then languorously licked away the sweat that trickled between her breasts.

After that, he began to thrust in and out of her, his hands grasping her buttocks, arching her hips to meet his own. She wrapped her legs around his, enfolding him, taking him deep inside her as she felt the tide start to surge once more within her, pounding, breaking, the combers sweeping through her body. Knowing she had achieved her peak, Nick sought his own, rough and urgent now, his fingers tightening upon her bruisingly as he shuddered long and hard against her. Then he collapsed atop her, his face buried in her hair, his breath coming in harsh pants in her ear.

"Wasn't it freezing in here a little while ago?" he asked after a long minute.

"Yes...but that was before you came in and heated things up," Caroline murmured sassily, her heart still thrumming.

"Believe me, if I'd known this was what would happen, I'd have broken the furnace myself the first day we got here," Nick declared, grinning insolently at her. Withdrawing, he rolled over on to his back, pulling her into the cradle of his arms. "So much for an annulment. You're stuck with me now."

Caroline wasn't sure how to take that, what he intended by it, and she was afraid to ask, afraid to discover he was only joking. So she said simply, softly, "I guess I won't mind *too* much. I mean, at least I know I'll be kept warm during our long, cold Minnesota winters."

"Count on it," he rejoined, his arm tightening around her possessively.

After a while, when the fire had begun to die down and the bedroom to grow chilly again, Nick rose to toss more logs onto the blaze, until it once more burned brightly. Then he returned to bed to set Caroline herself aflame again—until she felt like a wildfire, burning out of control.

Twelve

When Caroline awoke in the morning, she thought at first that she had only dreamed about Nick making love to her so passionately last night. She was alone in bed, and there was no blaze burning in the fireplace. Then, after a moment, she became aware that she was totally naked and that the hearth was filled with cold ashes. So she knew her marriage that was supposed to have been in name only had indeed been consummated.

Nick must have got up early. There wasn't even an indentation on the pillow on his side of the bed to show where he had slept. And strangely, the bedroom door was closed. That fact puzzled and unsettled Caroline, as she had not been in the habit of closing it at night, in case Nick should require the bathroom. For an instant, all sorts of wild imaginings ran through her mind. The chief of these was that having seduced her, making an annulment impossible, he had returned to Minnesota without her—to gloat over her gullibility, his bonus money for wedding her, and whatever else he hoped to get from their eventual divorce. She wondered if before boarding the corporate jet for their honeymoon, he had ever signed their prenuptial agreement.

Abruptly, Caroline felt cold and sick inside. What if she was right and Nick was worse than Paul Andersen had ever been—and she had made a total fool of herself again? She didn't want to believe any of this about her husband, or herself, either. Still, she could not think why he would have left her alone after last night, shutting the bedroom door behind him—so she wouldn't hear him sneaking from the cabin, no doubt!

Oh, God, why had she ever drunk that brandy-laced tea last night, let him make love to her? Her grandmother would be so furious and disappointed in her, her father angry and disapproving.

Shaking a little, Caroline rose from the bed to make her way to the bathroom. There, a vast sense of relief flooded her being when she spied Nick's toilet articles on the counter. If he had vamoosed, he surely would not have left those behind. Hard on the heels of her relief came shock when she glimpsed her reflection in the mirror. She looked like a…a *wanton,* she thought, like a woman who had not only been made love to recently—but also thoroughly and well.

Her long, sable hair was a mass of tangles around her face. Crescent smudges from lack of sleep shadowed her eyes. Her mouth was still slightly swollen and red from Nick's kisses. Faint marks on her throat, breasts, hips and thighs, made her blush as she remembered how he had kissed and stroked every part of her last night, driving her wild.

Until now, Caroline had always considered herself somewhat shy and reserved in bed, afraid of not being gorgeous or sexy enough to please. Maybe Nick hadn't made good his escape, but he hadn't hung around for more this morning, either, she thought glumly. Maybe she hadn't lived up to his expectations. She couldn't help but remember that when she had shoved a drunken Paul Andersen out her door for the last time, he had shouted terrible insults at her— the primary of which had been that she was frigid and lousy in bed. Maybe Nick had found her so, too. Why else would he have closed the bedroom door against her?

Reaching into the shower, Caroline turned on the taps, then stepped inside, feeling as though she might burst into tears at any moment. She was so lost in her miserable reverie and the running water was loud enough that she didn't hear Nick come into the bathroom. So she jumped, startled, when he opened the shower door and joined her—as naked as she.

"Nick! What're you—what're you doing?" She was stunned by his appearance and made a halfhearted attempt to cover herself.

"Taking a shower with my bride. God, I thought those two maintenance men would *never* finish fixing the furnace and get the hell out of here! I don't know which one was worse—the old one who practically talked my ear off, or the young one I caught staring into the bedroom at you. *He's* lucky I didn't tear his damned Peeping Tom head off—and if you hadn't been covered up, I would have!''

''You—you mean that's why you left me, why you closed the bedroom door on me?''

''Of course. Why? What other reason would there have been?'' Nick gazed down at her curiously, pushing a strand of hair back from her face.

''I don't know. I thought...I thought maybe I might have...disappointed you in some way,'' Caroline confessed softly. ''That you had found me—frigid or something.''

He swore at that—in Russian—but still, she knew it was a curse word he uttered. Putting his hand under her chin, he tipped her face up to his. ''This is something that damned fool Andersen said to you, isn't it? Isn't it, Caro?''

She nodded mutely.

''That bastard! I'd like to teach him a well-deserved lesson! Now, you listen to me, baby—and you listen good. There are no frigid women, only incompetent, insensitive men—and I don't think I'm one of those. Last night was wonderful...for both of us, I thought. I had hoped you felt the same.''

''I did. I do,'' Caroline murmured.

''Then, let's see, exactly where did we leave off last night?'' Pressing her up against the shower wall, he slowly lowered his mouth to hers, his eyes darkening with passion, his arousal plain as the warm water continued to pour down upon them both.

After they returned home from Maplewood Lodge, Caroline and Nick spent the rest of the weekend moving most of her clothes and favorite possessions into his house on the lake. This process was marred by their first quarrel, when she insisted on separate bedrooms.

"Damn it, Caro!" Nick's dark eyes were puzzled—and even hurt, she thought. But of course, her refusal to share his bed must be a blow to his ego, after their honeymoon. "I thought we had settled all this."

"Why... because that hot toddy you fixed me muddled my senses? Look, Nick, I'm not saying that what... what happened between us wasn't wonderful—because it was. It's simply that with everything that's occurred and how fast, I'm—I'm just not sure of my feelings at the moment, that's all. I—I need some time, some space, to try to sort things out in my mind. Ours was supposed to be a marriage of convenience. Our so-called honeymoon changed all that in a way I wasn't expecting. I didn't plan on... on becoming involved with you, and I'm just not cut out for a—a casual affair. Under the circumstances, what we did was extremely careless and irresponsible."

"Careless? Irresponsible? In what way?" He raised one brow inquiringly. "What do you mean, Caro?"

"Well, we didn't . . ." Her voice trailed away awk-wardly. She wasn't used to discussing such intimate details with a man. But he had to know. Taking a deep breath, she forced herself to continue. "Nick, I'm sure you probably assumed . . . well, that I'm on the pill or something. But I'm not, and we didn't . . . do any-thing for birth control . . . ."

"So what you're trying to tell me is that you could be pregnant now. Is that it?"

"Yes." She nodded, biting her lower lip anxiously at the thought. "Nick, as soon as your problems with the INS are worked out, we're going to be divorced. You know that. I know it. So a child would be a ter-rible complication, an innocent victim in all this. We just can't take that risk. It wouldn't be fair to either of us—and most of all, it wouldn't be fair to a child."

"Yeah, you're right, of course," he said slowly af-ter a long moment, a muscle throbbing in his taut jaw. "I'm sorry, baby. I just didn't think."

"Please don't imagine I'm blaming you for that, Nick, because I'm not. I'm as much at fault for what happened as you are. After all, you gave me a chance to draw back, and I didn't take it. But I am now. I'm sorry, too, but I think it's best if we . . . if we just for-get about what happened up in Canada."

"If that's what you want."

"It . . . it is," she lied, turning away so he wouldn't see the tears that stung her eyes. Because what she *truly* wanted was for theirs to become a real marriage, filled with love and children and family holiday traditions. She hoped he would take her in his arms and tell her he wanted that, too. But he didn't.

Instead, he said quietly, "Okay, Caro. You got it. I understand." Then he carried her luggage upstairs, turning right at the top of the steps, so she knew he was taking it into the bedroom at the opposite end of the hall from his own.

Her heart sank at the realization. Blinking back her tears, she almost ran up the stairs after him to tell him she had changed her mind, that he should take her belongings to his own bedroom. But determinedly, she fought the wild impulse. Sex with Nick *had* been wonderful. She had not lied about that. But that's all it had been, just sex. Beyond desire and gratitude, he had no feelings for her, and if she did for him, well, then she must strive to get them under control before she wound up being hurt, her heart broken again.

Still, the fact that she would not be sleeping with Nick, cradled in his warm embrace at night, depressed Caroline. It was with a heavy sigh that she slowly trudged upstairs to begin putting away her clothes and other possessions.

Down the hall in his own room, Nick flung himself down despondently onto his bed. His hands beneath his head, he stared up at the ceiling unseeingly. All he had thought about all day was making love to Caroline again. She was his wife, damn it! He had every right to sleep with her! And while he knew that her reasons for refusing him were valid, he couldn't help but wonder if she had told him the truth.

What single woman these days wasn't on some form of birth control? There were any number of methods available. And if she truly weren't, then why in the hell hadn't she mentioned that fact before letting him make love to her in their cabin at Maplewood Lodge? Nick could only think Caroline had lied to him, that this was her way of politely distancing herself from him, that perhaps she had only been amusing herself with him at the cabin.

Maybe when they had returned to Minneapolis, she had begun to have second thoughts, to think he wasn't good enough for her—or, more likely, for her family. After all, what was he, in reality, but a hired husband? Bought and paid for by the Fortunes so he wouldn't be deported before Kate's secret youth formula could be brought to fruition. Hell. If not for that, Nick would be willing to bet that Caroline would never have agreed to become his wife. He wouldn't have cared—except that like a fool, he had gone and fallen for his bride. Fallen like the proverbial ton of bricks.

She was everything he had ever wanted in a woman: beautiful, intelligent, creative and sophisticated—but without the hard edge that characterized a lot of successful women. Instead, she had a sweetness and shyness about her that gave her a softly feminine appeal. The more he had been around her, the more he had come to realize that. Deep down inside, she was terribly vulnerable.

She had let him close to her for a moment. Now, like a cautious little hermit crab, she had retreated back into her shell. But he could win her back, Nick thought, if he was careful and patient. Because there was no way he was going to lose his wife. No matter what she believed, a divorce was totally out of the question.

If necessary, to hold on to her, he was willing to have trouble with the INS for years!

Thirteen

In fact, trouble with the INS was precisely what Nick encountered first thing Monday morning. Two immigration agents were waiting for him in his administrative office off the laboratory at Fortune Cosmetics. They had made themselves comfortable in the chairs before his desk, but at his entrance, they stood, flipping out their leather identification wallets.

"Dr. Valkov? Lyndon Howard, Immigration and Naturalization Service. And this is Brody Sheffield. We'd like to speak with you if we may."

"Of course, gentlemen," Nick said, shaking their hands. "Won't you please be seated?"

They resumed the same chairs they had vacated just moments before. Howard, who was obviously the senior agent, cleared his throat. Then, reaching into the inside pocket of his suit jacket, he produced a pair of glasses and an envelope, from which he removed a letter. Putting on the bifocals, he glanced down at the missive.

"Dr. Valkov, I believe you received a copy of this letter some days ago from the INS, in which you were instructed to appear at our office here locally to surrender your green card and undergo deportation procedures, did you not?''

''Yes, I did.''

''Then . . . may I inquire as to why you did *not* follow our instructions?''

''Because I was getting married at the time,'' Nick explained affably, although his eyes were alert and wary. ''And according to my legal counsel, that makes it impossible for you to deport me, no matter how much you may wish to do so.''

''That's not exactly true, Dr. Valkov—as I'm sure your lawyer must also have informed you. You see, if the INS has reason to believe your marriage is one of convenience, in name only, for the sole sake of preventing your deportation, we can declare it invalid and eject you from the United States, anyway.''

''Yes, I understand that. However, what *you* must understand is that my wife and I had been seeing each other for some time and had planned to be married sometime later this year—a rather large wedding with all the trimmings, to which we were both very much looking forward. I'm afraid your letter was most upsetting to her, since as a result, we were compelled to get married rather hastily at the courthouse instead.''

''Indeed?'' Howard's tone indicated his skepticism. ''Quite a nice story, Dr. Valkov. I'm sure you won't have any objections to us checking it out.''

''Not at all. In fact, if you'd like, I can have my wife join us right now.''

"Please do."

Picking up the receiver of the telephone on his desk, Nick punched in Caroline's extension number. "Sweetheart? It's me. Are you terribly busy at the moment? Because I have a couple of INS agents sitting in my office, and they'd like to talk to you. So I'd really appreciate if you'd join us. Great. I'll see you shortly, then." He hung up, then turned back to Howard and Sheffield. "She's on her way down."

"Fine. In the meantime, I hope you won't mind answering some questions for us?"

"Not at all."

"Good. Take notes, Brody," Howard directed his partner. "Now, Dr. Valkov, how did you meet your wife?"

"Through our work here at Fortune Cosmetics. She's the vice president of marketing. We...ah...literally ran into each other one day in a corridor while we were on our way to a meeting. I was attracted to her. I hoped she might feel the same way toward me, and I offered to cook dinner for her one evening."

"And did she accept your invitation?"

"She did. I drove her out to my house on the lake, where I prepared a simple supper consisting of a salad, French bread and beef Stroganoff. Afterward, we shared a glass of wine and listened to music. Tchaikovsky, as I recall."

"And how long ago did all this take place?"

"Oh, I don't know for sure. Quite some time ago, though, several months at least," Nick lied.

"And you've been seeing her steadily since then?"

"That's right."

"And when did you become engaged?"

"Shortly before I received your letter, actually. Ah, Caro, there you are, sweetheart." Rising from the chair, Nick came around his desk to take her in his arms and kiss her lightly on the mouth. "This is Mr. Howard and Mr. Sheffield—from the INS. Gentlemen, this is my wife, Caroline Fortune Valkov."

"Fortune!" Sheffield exclaimed, his eyes widening as he glanced anxiously at his superior, wondering abruptly if they had, after all, made a mistake.

"Yes, that's right," Caroline confirmed coolly as she shook hands with the two men. "I'm Kate Fortune's eldest granddaughter and—as I'm sure Nick's told you—the vice president of marketing here at Fortune Cosmetics." Normally, all this was not information she readily volunteered. Under the circumstances, however, she felt it prudent to impress the agents with her family and wealth. By wedding Nick to prevent his deportation, she had technically broken the law and could be fined at the very least.

"I'm sorry if we've interrupted your schedule, Mrs. Valkov. However, I'm sure you understand our need to ask you a few questions. If you'd please be seated." Howard motioned toward the chairs.

"Yes, of course." Crossing the floor, Caroline took a seat as close to Nick as possible, her pulse racing, even though she and Nick had rehearsed this scene several times.

She wished her hair were up in a French twist, that she had her glasses to hide behind, that she were dressed in a tailored Chanel suit instead of the jazzy Versace ensemble her sister Allie had talked her into buying during a shopping trip once and that Nick had insisted on her wearing today. She hadn't an inkling of the fact that she looked as good, if not better, than Cindy Crawford on a great day—and that despite their suspicions, the two INS agents were already sitting there thinking that with her looks and money, Nick would have been out of his mind *not* to have married her.

Howard proceeded with the interview, asking Caroline several of the same questions he had already asked Nick. Much to her relief, she knew from Nick's encouraging smile that she was doing fine, that she hadn't made any mistakes in her half truths.

"Now, Mrs. Valkov, forgive me for prying into such a personal matter, but I have to ask this next question because generally in the case of a couple wedding merely to prevent the deportation of one of them, the marriage is in name only, so a quick annulment can be obtained later. So, will you tell me please, has your marriage been consummated?"

Caroline could feel the crimson heat that flamed in her cheeks at that. Not trusting herself to speak, she nodded, embarrassed—wondering, stricken, if this information would somehow now get back to her grandmother and father.

"In fact, we just returned from our honeymoon," Nick announced blandly. "We spent a week at Maplewood Lodge, just across the Canadian border. I can give you the address and telephone number if you'd like to check that out, too. They'll remember us, I'm sure. We had the honeymoon cabin—and our furnace broke down the last night we were there."

"Yes, thank you, I *would* appreciate having that information," Howard replied as he got to his feet. "However, I don't think there'll be a problem with your marriage. If we need anything further, we'll be in touch."

"You know where to find us." Nick handed to Howard a slip of paper containing the address and telephone number of Maplewood Lodge. "Oh, and one more thing. I don't know how or where you got the impression that I was ever an agent for the KGB. I'm a chemist—and *only* a chemist. That's all I've ever been. Think about it. If I really *were* a spy for Russia, why would I be wasting my time here at a cosmetics company, for pity's sake? Do you really believe I'm hiding transmitters in lipstick tubes? Miniature cameras in compacts? That I'm talking to Moscow on a shoe phone? Maybe you think I call Caro 'Ninety-nine,' too? Because if you do, I'd say you've been watching too many old reruns of *Get Smart.*''

Sheffield chuckled, but cut the sound off immediately at a sharp, annoyed glance from Howard. ''It may be a joke to you, Dr. Valkov, but we Americans take our security seriously. You newlyweds have a nice day, now.''

Once the two men had gone, Caroline rose to go to Nick's side, her face anxious as she laid one hand upon his arm. ''Do you really think they believed us? That Mr. Howard spoke the truth about there not being any trouble about our marriage?''

''I don't know. But they'll have one hell of a time trying to prove us liars—and they know it. You all but told them they'd be taking on the entire Fortune family and empire, Caro. That would be a daunting prospect to most anybody, especially here in the Twin Cities. Thank you, sweetheart.'' Nick bent his head and kissed her.

When she didn't at first protest or pull away, he increased the pressure of his mouth upon hers, his tongue compelling her lips to open, insinuating itself inside. Caroline's mouth clung to his as a rush of desire surged through her. He tasted of hot, black morning coffee and Player's cigarettes, things she had come to associate with him. He smelled of soap and cologne and cigarette smoke. His tongue twisted and twined with her own. His hands snarled in her thick, shiny mass of sable hair.

As he pulled her close, she could feel the strength and hardness of his arousal pressed against her. In moments, he would be locking his office door, laying her down upon his sofa or the floor. And she wanted that. But she must not give in to temptation.

"Nick...Nick, no..." she murmured, resolutely pushing herself away from him, placing her trembling hands against his broad chest to hold him at bay. "I...I have to get back to work, and so do you. My coming down here to deal with the INS has already wreaked havoc on my schedule. Mary had to cancel an appointment I had and reschedule another one. Besides, don't you think the rumor mills are already working overtime as it is?"

"Yeah, I suppose so." Reluctantly, he released her, smiling ruefully—although his dark eyes smoldered like twin embers as they raked her.

She was right. In their absence, the gossip had flown thick and fast at Fortune Cosmetics. Both Caroline and Nick had known that when they had walked into the office building earlier this morning. People had eyed them speculatively everywhere: in the parking garage, the elevator, the corridors. More than one person had called, "Hey, I heard you two got married," clearly hoping to be enlightened with the truth.

Nick had answered nobody, merely grinned like the proverbial cat that had swallowed the canary, while Caroline had blushed with embarrassment that she should once more be an object of gossip at the company.

"Oh, I almost forgot." She turned back from the door as she was leaving his office. "Grandmother wants us to have lunch with her in her office at noon. I guess we should probably tell her about the INS visit."

"Yeah, we should—because although they seem satisfied at the moment, you never know. They may be back."

"I certainly hope not," Caro declared fervently. "One interrogation was more than enough for me! See you at lunch." She strode from his office, haunted by the strange sensation that Nick was watching her walk away—and admiring the sway of her backside.

She would *not* look back over her shoulder, she told herself sternly. She would not.

He was leaning against the doorjamb of his office, his hands shoved into his trouser pockets, his gaze such that anyone glancing at him must have known what he was thinking as he watched her. When she peeked back over her shoulder at him, he grinned wickedly, his eyes dancing. Then he called out something to her in Russian. Caroline didn't know what— but she *was* sure it had been quite naughty.

She devoutly hoped no one in the laboratory spoke Russian.

Fourteen

Caroline and Nick's days soon settled into a pattern. They rose early, taking turns preparing breakfast for each other, which they lingered over, reading the newspaper and watching CNN. Then, in the Mercedes-Benz, he drove them to the office, insisting that there was no need for them to take two cars into the city.

"I worry about you when the country roads are icy like this, Caro," he declared gravely, stroking her hair lightly. "I don't want you out on them alone, especially after dark."

On the days when one or both of them worked late hours, they stayed overnight in the city, in Caroline's old apartment—where Nick now had as many clothes hanging in the closets as she did. Otherwise, they returned home to his house on the lake, which she had come to adore and to which she had, here and there, added little touches of her own, so it was not so masculine as before. She and Nick usually wound up fixing supper together, after which they played cards or board games or listened to music or read aloud to each other by the fire in the living room. To Caroline's amazement, Nick loved the classics and poetry as much as she did.

"Why should you find that surprising?" he asked when she mentioned it.

"Well, because most people today don't seem to read the classics much anymore—and poetry hardly at all."

"Then they don't know what they're missing, do they? Some of the most beautiful ideas in the world are in those books, expressed in language that has a rhythm and music—a soul—all its own. What shall we have tonight? Wordsworth or Tennyson?"

"Tennyson, please. *Idylls of the King.*"

So he read to her in his deep, rich voice, while she sat before the fire and sipped her wine and allowed herself to be transported to another time, another place.

At the office, they continued their work on the secret youth formula, Caroline finalizing the details of the marketing campaign, Nick completing his tests in the laboratory. Sometimes, it seemed they were the only two people left in the Fortune Cosmetics building after five o'clock. Whenever that happened, more often than not, Nick would appear in her office with cartons of Chinese food or Italian, which they would eat at her desk before returning to their respective jobs.

Caroline had never been quite so happy in her life— or so despairing. Despite all her best intentions, how hard she had tried to keep her distance from Nick, to hold on to her heart, she had lost it to him. She didn't know how she could have let such a thing happen. This was surely not what her grandmother and father had meant to occur when they had suggested she marry Nick. Yet she was ready to risk their disapproval, to defy them both, if only she believed her husband could love her, would ever come to do so.

But there was no hope of that, Caroline thought disheartened. Nick treated her as a caring husband would his wife only because he had promised her grandmother he would do so—and he didn't want to risk losing his job or his freedom. He didn't want to be deported, that was all. And if he sometimes forgot himself and kissed Caroline as she were truly his wife and attempted to persuade her to share his bed again, well, that was only the physical attraction he felt toward her, the chemistry at which he was so brilliant.

She simply *had* to put all this from her head, Caroline told herself sternly now. Their relationship was interfering with her work. She couldn't concentrate on what she was supposed to be doing at Fortune Cosmetics. Twice, she had been late for meetings, and once, she had forgotten one entirely. She could only feel relief that somehow her grandmother hadn't learned about the sloppiness of her schedule lately.

Tucking the folder she carried under one arm and tossing the diet cola she had just finished drinking into one of the nearby recycling bins, Caroline headed back toward her office. She had spent all morning going over more artwork for the magazine layouts for Fabulous Face. As a result, she probably had a pile of papers stacked high on her desk by now, she thought, sighing. And she had missed lunch, too. She would have to get a sandwich from one of the snack machines or something.

"Caroline! Caroline, wait up!"

Oh, God, she groaned inwardly as she glanced back over her shoulder and spied Paul Andersen coming after her down the corridor. She looked around, hoping to see another employee or two, but the hall was empty at the moment. Because of that, she kept on walking.

"Caroline!" Catching up with her, he grabbed her arm, pulling her to a stop. "I know you heard me calling you, so why didn't you wait up like I asked?"

"Possibly because I don't want to talk to you, Paul. As far as I'm concerned, we have nothing to say to each other—now, or ever! So let go of my arm!"

"Look, don't give me the cold shoulder. I only want a few minutes of your time, that's all. You owe me that much, I think."

"I don't owe you anything. Let go, I said." With a jerk, Caroline wrenched her arm free and started on down the corridor again. From the smell of his breath, she suspected Paul had had a very old-fashioned, three-martini lunch, that he somehow hadn't got the message that these days club soda or mineral water was de rigueur. And remembering his drunken behavior that night at her apartment, she wasn't about to hang around for a repeat performance. "If you don't stop bothering me, Paul, I'm going to call security," she insisted when he followed her.

"I just want to know whether or not it's true that you've married Nick Valkov."

"Whether I have or not, it's none of your business, Paul."

"It is! Damn it, Caroline! You were my fiancée once. I thought...that is, I had *hoped* that you might be again someday. I know your family poisoned you against me, insisting I was only after your money. But that wasn't true."

"Wasn't it?"

"No."

"Why don't I buy that, Paul? Now, go away and leave me alone!"

"You're wearing a set of wedding rings, Caroline. So who are you trying to fool? Do you know what people are saying behind your back? That your family paid Nick to marry you, that they hired you a husband because you couldn't get a man any other way! What I want to know is...why him? What's the difference between him and me? I at least loved you, Caroline, in my own fashion."

"You're despicable," she said icily, mortified by what Paul told her. Surely, he was making this gossip up—or worse, more likely, he had started it himself!

He was malicious enough to have done something like that for revenge, she thought. Oh, God. It had never occurred to her that everyone at the company might learn that her father had paid Nick to marry her. It simply *had* to be a guess on Paul's part, rumors he had spread out of sheer spite. And she didn't know how to counteract them.

Caroline had reached her own office now, but Paul was still behind her, babbling away half drunkenly. He seized her arm again, and this time, she couldn't pull free.

"Paul, you're hurting me," she told him quietly. She could see her secretary, Mary, sitting at her desk beyond Caroline's office, speaking into the telephone receiver. Caroline didn't want a witness to an ugly scene—and further gossip being bandied about the halls of Fortune Cosmetics. "I think you'd better go. Mary is probably calling security," she lied, because in truth, she didn't know whom her secretary was talking to.

She found out only moments later when Nick stepped out of the elevator across from her office, his face as dark as a thundercloud.

"Take your damned hands off my wife, Andersen, or you'll be sorry!" he growled, striding toward Paul angrily.

"Nick!" Caroline cried, vastly relieved to see her husband. "He's been drinking," she said, by way of explaining Paul's behavior to Nick.

She thought the two men would come to blows, but her former fiancé proved too cowardly for that. Glancing over her shoulder and spying her husband, his eyes widened, and he abruptly turned and hurried away down the corridor. Nick would have pursued him, but Caroline grasped her husband's hand, drawing him back.

"No, let him go. Please, Nick. It's enough that you got rid of him."

"Are you all right, baby?"

"Yes. He was only making a pest out of himself."

"I don't care." A muscle twitched alarmingly in Nick's set jaw. "If your secretary hadn't phoned me to let me know what was happening up here, he might have hurt you. I'm going upstairs right now and have Kate fire him. That bastard doesn't deserve to work here after all he's done to you—and this is the last straw! I'm sure your grandmother will agree."

Nothing Caroline said dissuaded Nick from this course of action.

"Don't argue with me about this, baby. I won't stand for it. Andersen tried to rape you once before, and it's obvious he still has both feelings toward you and a drinking problem. You often work late hours, when you're the only person on this entire floor. What if he came up here some night and attacked you? Who would hear you scream? No, I won't have it, and that's final, Caroline!"

Her grandmother, hearing all Nick had to report, sternly agreed.

"Why didn't you tell me about Paul before, Caroline?" she asked soberly. "Had I known, I would never have permitted him to continue working here." Picking up her telephone receiver, she called down to Paul's department head and instructed him tersely to fire Paul immediately. Then she hung up and turned back to the newlyweds. "Nick, I want to thank you for coming up here to tell me about Paul. I truly appreciate it. It makes me shudder just to think he might actually have harmed my granddaughter in some way."

"Caro's my wife, Kate. It's my duty to keep her safe."

His duty, Caroline thought bleakly. Of course. Why should there have been any other reason besides him doing the right thing by her, as he had promised he would?

"So. How are you two newlyweds getting along?" Kate inquired.

"Fine. Just fine," Nick replied. "Caro's moved into my house on the lake, and in just weeks, she's managed to turn it into a real home. We've got our schedules worked out nicely, so I can drive us back and forth to work every day and Caro's not out on the country roads after dark. And so far, the INS hasn't paid us any more visits."

"Excellent." Kate smiled, although her eyes were thoughtful as she gazed at Caroline, noting her silence. "And how about my secret youth formula? I hate to sound like a tired old parrot, harping on the same thing over and over. But to tell you the truth, I'm just so excited about Fabulous Face that I can hardly contain myself."

Nick grinned wryly. "Yes, I've gathered, Kate. So, although we're not yet done with our testing, I'll give you a brief update. We are now almost certain that Ingredient X is going to prove to be a plant rumored to grow only in the Amazon jungle. Its Latin name is *floris virginis*—maiden flower. But the Indians in South America call it the youth flower, and it's the properties they describe it as having that we're interested in. However, at the moment, we're not even sure it really exists. The stories told about it may be only that—stories, legends, myths, whatever. So we need to do some further investigation before we go off on a wild-goose chase. Currently, we're testing other plants with properties supposedly similar to those of the maiden flower, to see if we're even on the right track. Still, my gut instinct tells me that we are—so don't be surprised if, in the near future, I come to you with a request to take a small team down to the Amazon, Kate."

"No, I won't," she responded calmly. But inwardly, she was turning cartwheels as she thought, *However, that isn't going to prove necessary, because now that I know what you're after, I intend to fly down to South America and get it myself!*

Shortly afterward, blissfully unaware of Kate's plans, Caroline and Nick left Kate's office, walking together down the corridor toward the elevators. Before they had reached them, however, Nick suddenly caught hold of his wife's hand and drew her into a small conference room off to one side. It was empty and dark—and didn't grow much brighter when he flicked on the lights. Apparently, it had last been used for either a video or slide presentation, and the dimmer switch was set on low, so the illumination provided by the recessed lights in the ceiling was scant. To her surprise, however, Nick made no move to turn the lights up, and he closed the door and locked it.

"Nick, what're you doing? Why did you bring me in here? Is there something wrong?"

"You tell me. I was just about to ask you that same question."

"I—I don't understand...."

"You barely had two words to say in your grandmother's office, Caro. Because of that, she's worried that you're unhappy with me, I could tell. *Are* you unhappy? Is there something I've said, something I've done to make you so? Are you mad at me for getting that bastard Andersen fired? Are you—God forbid—still in love with him?"

"No...no, it's nothing like that."

"Then, what is it? What's wrong?"

"Nothing. Why should there be anything the matter?"

"I don't know. That's what I'm trying to find out. And I have the strangest feeling that you're lying to me, baby—and I don't like that. I don't like it at all. If it's not Andersen, then is there someone else?"

"No, of course not." But to her dismay, Caroline found she couldn't look her husband in the eye when she answered, she was so afraid he would see that she indeed *wasn't* telling him the truth, that there *was* someone else—him!

"Caroline. Caroline, look at me, damn it!" Catching her chin with his hand, he forced her mute, stubbornly resisting face up to his. "I thought we agreed that we wouldn't see anybody else for the duration of our marriage."

"Yes, we did. And I'm not, I swear."

"Good—because I've changed my mind. I *won't* turn a blind eye. You're my wife—and I didn't like seeing you with that slime Andersen's hands all over you!" Nick's eyes blazed with anger at the memory as he stared down at her. The muscle in his taut jaw flexed.

Despite herself, Caroline felt a tiny thrill shoot through her. Why, he was behaving as though he were jealous! What if he was? That would mean he had begun to feel *something* toward her, even if it was not yet love. No matter how hard she tried to rein in her emotions, her heart soared at the thought. Was it possible that Nick was falling in love with her, as she had him?

"Paul wanted to know if you and I were really married," she stated quietly. "It seems he harbored hopes, still, of wedding me himself. And when I wouldn't answer him, he said something about my wedding rings and that...everybody at Fortune Cosmetics knew my family had...paid you to marry me, that I...couldn't get a husband any other way."

"Oh, Caro, you know that's not true," Nick insisted, pulling her into his arms, kissing her and stroking her hair lightly.

"Maybe not, but still, it's embarrassing and humiliating to think Paul was spreading rumors like that about me, to think there are those at the company who might have believed him." Tears stung her eyes at the thought.

"Shhh. Nobody will have taken seriously anything he said. They'll put it down to sour grapes—and rightly so. No one knows the truth about our marriage, baby—and I for damned sure better not hear anybody say I'm nothing but a hired husband!"

"But it's true," Caroline murmured.

"Is that *really* how you think of me, Caro? Is that the real reason why you wouldn't sleep with me again after we came back from Canada?"

"No...oh, no, Nick. I didn't mean that the way it sounded. I—I meant that it's true that my family paid you to marry me, that you...probably wouldn't have wanted me, otherwise."

Understanding dawned in Nick's eyes. "Is that what all this is about, Caro? Is that what's troubling you? Because if it is, you can just get that idea out of your head right now. Hell. I've been attracted to you, interested in taking you out, for ages—only you never would give me the time of day until your family needed me to save your grandmother's secret youth formula. Otherwise, we'd have been dating a long time ago. Baby, don't you know what you do to me?" he asked softly before his eyes darkened with passion and his mouth took hers.

There was nothing tentative or tender about his kiss. It was rough, urgent, taking Caroline's breath and leaving her blood roaring in her ears, her heart pounding so hard that she thought it would burst in her breast. She clung to Nick as he bent her back, shoving aside a chair and pressing her down upon the conference table, his mouth moving hard and hungrily on hers. A wild, electric shudder jolted through her. Desire flooded her being. Her fingers tightened into fists in his thick, dark hair, as, moaning, she opened her lips to him, her tongue meeting his own, tasting and twining.

Her response seemed to inflame Nick. He tore at her sweater, jerking it up, then pushing up her bra, too, to free her breasts. His palms cupped them possessively, caressing and kneading, his thumbs teasing her nipples to tautly furled buds. His mouth swept down to capture one flushed peak, sucking greedily as she whimpered and writhed beneath him. She could feel his hands sliding up her legs, pushing up her skirt. Caroline thought panty hose were one of the most uncomfortable pieces of underwear ever invented— second only to the archaic corset—so she followed the French custom of wearing thigh-high stockings.

Nick hadn't known that until now, but the realization drove him wild with both desire and jealousy. It was something secret and sexy he had discovered about his wife. He would never see her at the office again without thinking about the fact that beneath her skirt, she was wearing only a pair of thigh-high stockings and wispy, French-cut panties. The thought that whenever she crossed her legs in her office, at a conference table, in the executive dining room, another man might glimpse the top of a stocking, a flash of thigh, incensed him, made him long to insist that she wear nothing but sober, calf-length skirts to work from now on.

He told her as much—but to his surprise and irritation, Caroline only laughed.

"Why, what's this sudden change of heart, Nick?" she teased, still smiling. "*You* were the one who said I needed to try some designers like Versace, Hervé Leger and Badgley Mischka. Besides, can I help it if skirts are everything from minis to maxis these days?"

"No, I guess not. But damn it, Caroline! I don't want other guys knowing my wife goes around in thigh-high stockings all day!"

"Well, *I'm* certainly not going to tell them, Nick." Caroline's pulse raced as she gazed up at him. He *was* jealous. She lowered her lashes to conceal her thoughts. "I didn't realize you found thigh-high stockings so objectionable. I'll buy some panty hose, if you like."

"I don't like," he growled, his tongue tracing the outline of her mouth before he kissed her deeply again. His teeth caught her lower lip gently before his mouth seared across her cheek, her temple, the strands of her hair. "Because then I couldn't do this," he muttered huskily in her ear, his hand slipping beneath the inset of her panties, making her gasp. "You're all wet, sweetheart. I think you want me. What do you think?" When she didn't respond, turning her head away and blushing, he laughed softly.

Then, deliberately, he began to stroke her—languorous, circling, taunting caresses that excited her unbearably but did nothing to bring her release. Whimpering, her head thrashing at the hollow, burning ache that had seized her, she pushed against his hand, wanting, *needing* to be filled by him. But he refused to assuage her with his fingers, continuing to torment her, bringing her to the edge of climax again and again, only to leave her unsated.

And all the while, he kissed her, his tongue delving deep into her mouth, laving her breasts and nipples, until she was frantic, sobbing. She tried desperately to unbutton his shirt, to unzip his trousers. But to her distress, Nick caught her wrists with his free hand, determinedly pinioning them above her head, so she was helpless against him.

"Nick . . . please . . ." she gasped out.

"Please, what, baby?"

"Make love to me."

"I am, sweetheart."

"No, you know what I mean, what I want, what I *need*—"

"Do I?" He laughed softly again, then kissed her, his warm breath fanning her face, her breasts. He sucked her nipples once more, tongue licking, swirling, as he went on fondling the tender, moist folds of her, the throbbing heart of her. "Do you want me inside you, Caroline? Is that it?" he asked hoarsely.

"Yes . . . *yes!*"

"All right." He unzipped his trousers to free himself then, so hard and hot for her that he didn't even slip her lacy panties off, just drew their inset to one side and drove into her. She came the minute he entered her, crying out and arching against him wildly, her orgasm so strong that Nick felt it, too, was maddened by it. Urgently, he thrust deeply into her, again and again, rocking her harder and faster until his own climax gripped him.

Afterward, he kissed her lingeringly, then slowly withdrew and zipped up his trousers. His eyes danced with deviltry, and a wicked smile curved his mouth as he stood there gazing down at her sprawled on the conference table. He took in her hair tangled around her face and her lips bruised and swollen from his kisses, her sweater and bra pushed up to reveal her naked breasts, her skirt wrinkled up around her bare thighs. She was gorgeous, Nick thought.

"Mrs. Valkov, I sincerely hope this is *not* the way you conduct all your meetings," he drawled lazily.

"Meetings! Oh, my God—" Caroline glanced at her watch frantically, jerking her bra and sweater down as she scrambled from the conference table. "I'm supposed to be in one in fifteen minutes! I can't believe this happened!" With trembling fingers, she combed her hair frenziedly. "We talked about this, Nick! That we wouldn't *do* this—"

"You didn't tell me to stop, Caro. In fact, as I recall, you begged me to continue."

"I shouldn't have. I *wouldn't* have, if you hadn't . . . if you hadn't—" She broke off abruptly, flushing and biting her lower lip. "No man should have such power over a woman. It's—it's indecent!"

"You loved it. *I* loved it. We'll do it again tonight."

"No, we won't," she insisted, wishing desperately that she had a mirror in which to check her appearance. She would have to hurry down to her office before her meeting, to make sure she didn't look like she had just made mad, passionate love on a conference table. *A conference table!* God, she would never see one again without thinking about what she and Nick had done here on this one. "We won't," she reiterated obstinately.

"We will," Nick insisted. "As you've just seen, I can be *very* persuasive."

Caroline didn't know what to say to that—because hadn't she just proved his boast true, that she couldn't resist his determined onslaught upon her body and senses? She should be ashamed, she told herself, for being so weak-willed. She should be even more ashamed at how his words excited her, at the way her heart was racing. To cover her confusion, she unlocked the conference-room door and stepped into the corridor beyond, Nick following.

To Caroline's utter horror, they ran into her grandmother just outside. Knowing it must be obvious to anyone in that moment what she and Nick had been up to, Caroline opened her mouth to speak, to apologize, but with an upraised hand, Kate silenced her.

"No, don't say anything. That way, I can pretend I didn't see the two of you." Kate's voice was wry, but a smile tugged at the corners of her mouth, and her eyes twinkled. "But newlyweds or not, don't let this happen again during business hours. Oh, and Nick, you may call me Grandmother if you wish." With these startling pronouncements, Kate strode on down the corridor, leaving Caroline standing there with her mouth agape.

"Grandmother wasn't angry," she murmured, astounded. "She didn't disapprove."

"Well, why in the hell should she? You're my wife, after all."

Fifteen

"Duckie," the low voice on the telephone growled as throatily as it had purred some weeks ago. "I am *not* happy, Duckie. I am not happy at all. You told me you had an acquaintance or two at the INS. You told me you would get rid of Dr. Nicolai Valkov for me. But he's still here, Duckie. And that has angered and displeased me so much that I'm afraid...yes, I'm very much afraid...that I'm not going to be able to see you anymore. You see, I don't like people who don't keep their word to me, Duckie. They simply can't be trusted."

This time, Senator Donald Devane wasn't leaning back in his big, burgundy-leather chair. Instead, he was hunched over his massive, antique oak desk, like a schoolboy preparing for a caning. He was sweating, but it wasn't because of any amorous feeling. It was because he was petrified. What if he never saw the owner of the husky voice again? Never saw the black boudoir ensemble? Or worse, had his discreet little affair exposed by an anonymous telephone call to the media. He had a wife and family at home—and the American public didn't appreciate faithlessness in their politicians. He was going to be up for reelection shortly.

Oh, God, he groaned inwardly. How had he ever fallen for that smoky voice, its seductive owner? He must have been drunk at the time—or totally out of his mind. What was he going to do? He simply *had* to save himself, his career!

"I—I can be trusted," he stammered, cursing how his voice squeaked and croaked, revealing his fear. He could almost see the slow, malicious smile that lit up the face at the other end of the telephone. "And I—I *will* get rid of Nick Valkov, just as I promised. It's—it's simply that things are a—a little more complicated, that's all. Nobody expected him to get married to save himself from deportation."

"Well, you *should* have expected it, you fool!" the voice snarled furiously in the senator's ear, making him shiver as he abruptly remembered all the pictures locked up in the bedroom safe that belonged to the voice. Images of those photographs appearing in the newspapers and on television haunted him horribly. "Nick Valkov is brilliant, one of the world's foremost chemists, for God's sake! Did you think he was simply going to stand idly by while the INS labeled him a suspected KGB agent and deported him?"

"N-n-no." Senator Devane yanked his handkerchief from his pocket to mop his profusely perspiring brow—and prayed his secretary wasn't listening at the door to his furtive conversation. "But—but who would ever have dreamed he would marry somebody like Caroline Fortune? Good God! He might as well have married one of the Kennedys or Rockefellers, the Kochs or Basses, the Hunts—"

"I *get* the picture, Duckie!" the voice snapped, incensed.

"But—but what do you expect me to *do?* The Fortune holdings comprise one of the largest Fortune 500 companies. Kate Fortune is one of the ten richest women in the United States! And Caroline is her eldest granddaughter. You told me nobody would care if Nick Valkov was deported," the senator dared to say accusingly.

"And nobody does—except for that dried-up old maid of a Fortune granddaughter. I've heard rumors that the Fortunes actually paid Nick Valkov to marry her, that she couldn't get a husband any other way. So theirs isn't a real marriage, by any means. It's all a fraud, to keep Nick Valkov from being deported! So don't take that tone with me, Duckie. I don't like it— and you know what happens when I don't like something, don't you?"

"Y-y-yes," he stuttered nervously, thinking of all the people in high places who had been brought low, thanks to the owner of the voice that had now turned as cold and hard as an iceberg. "But in all fairness, I *did* try to keep my word to you. And the INS *did* interrogate both Nick Valkov and Caroline Fortune.

Unfortunately, the two INS agents who conducted the interview were satisfied that the marriage *is* for real.''

"Well, *I'm* not! Not by a long shot! And it isn't, I tell you! It's a fake. So I suggest you use whatever influence you have with the INS to get Nick Valkov's file reopened as soon as possible. Because if you don't, Duckie, you're going to be very, very sorry. Do you understand?''

"Yes, yes, I do, I do." Senator Devane fumbled anxiously at his tie and loosened his collar, which felt as though it were choking him. "But you'll have to give me some time to take care of the matter. Given that the Fortunes are involved, things aren't going to happen overnight.''

"Don't worry about that. You're not the only resource at my disposal. I have others. So you see, Duckie, you're not indispensable. No one is. So you get on the phone to the INS first thing tomorrow morning. Otherwise, I'm going to have to make a few phone calls of my own, Duckie—to the press,'' the voice announced with feigned sweetness, then chuckled with spiteful glee before the line went dead, leaving the dial tone buzzing in the senator's ear.

After hanging up blindly, Senator Devane yanked open his desk drawer, searching frantically for the prescription bottle inside. Locating it at last, he ripped off the lid and popped one of the pills. His heart was hammering so horribly that he feared he was having an attack. He cursed the day he had ever set eyes on the owner of that wicked laugh. Tomorrow morning, he would call the INS. But tonight...tonight, he intended to get very drunk, so he could temporarily forget this dreadful mess he had got himself into.

Bending down in his chair, he opened the concealed pair of small doors set back under the knee-hole, removing a bottle of whiskey and a glass from the bar inside. With trembling, sweating hands, he poured a stiff drink and downed it in a single gulp.

If he didn't somehow get rid of Nick Valkov, he would be finished, Senator Devane thought. Utterly ruined, his career destroyed and his homelife in shambles. His wife would divorce him. His children would probably never speak to him again. He simply couldn't permit any of that to happen.

By hook or by crook, Nick Valkov had to go.

Sixteen

Minneapolis, Minnesota

It had taken many months of scheming, but there were always weak links in any chain: otherwise decent employees who had personal problems and desperately needed money, dissatisfied employees who harbored a secret grudge against their employers, and hate-filled ex-employees who had lost their jobs and now wanted nothing so much as to gain revenge upon their former employers. More than one of these links had been utilized—although the man who furtively let himself into the Fortune Cosmetics building didn't know that. The motives and methods of the person who had hired him didn't matter. All he knew or cared about was the fact that he was being paid a tidy sum for this night's work.

At a post office box obtained for mailing purposes, he had received a copy of the layout of the Fortune Cosmetics building, a timetable of the security personnel's and cleaning crew's schedules, and an identification card that permitted him access to the more sensitive areas of the company, such as the laboratory. This was his primary goal tonight. But first, he made his way to the basement, where he slipped through the regions that were the usual purview of the maintenance crews. There, after slipping his gear bag from his shoulder and laying it aside, he busied himself with shutting off the main valve that controlled the edifice's water supply.

The intruder didn't have much time now. At any moment, someone could discover that the building had lost its water. It might be put down to a city line rupturing. On the other hand, somebody might be bright or annoyed enough to call down to the basement to have maintenance check it out.

Hefting his gear bag over his shoulder, he hurried to the bank of service elevators, pushing the Up button. He glanced down at his wristwatch. It was just coming on midnight. He figured that all the employees ought to have gone home by now. Many of the cleaning crews would be winding up for the evening, as well. However, others would still be working, so, as a precaution, he wore a janitorial uniform. In his pocket, he carried a ski mask, in case he needed to hide his face. It wasn't likely that the need would arise, given the fact that he had the Fortune Cosmetics identification card. Still, it paid to be careful.

Recklessness was what got people caught—and put into prison.

An elevator came to a halt, its heavy doors sliding open to admit him. He relaxed his alert posture slightly when he saw that it was empty. Still, his adrenaline pumped wildly. There was always the chance that it might have had someone in it. He stepped inside, pressing the number of the floor on which the laboratory was located.

Despite the lateness of the house, Nick was ecstatic. Tonight's work represented a major breakthrough. He was positive, now, that the missing Ingredient X in Kate's secret youth formula was the mysterious maiden flower, to be found only in the Amazon rain forest, if at all. If not, if it turned out to be only a legend, a myth, there were other plants he could use. But his gut instinct told him the maiden flower was the one he really wanted.

Yawning, he slowly began to recheck the figures he had entered into the computer at the workstation he was using. Then he saved the information to the floppy diskette and pushed the release button, tucking the diskette into the pocket of his lab coat. After that, he put away all the apparatus he had used to run his tests that evening, then finished cleaning up the laboratory.

In his administrative office off the laboratory, he opened his wall safe and slipped the floppy diskette inside, then closed the heavy door and turned the dial a couple of times so it wouldn't be resting on the final number of the combination. He pocketed the key to the safe and switched off the lights in his office. Then he strolled from the laboratory into the corridor, where the bank of elevators for the upper floors was located.

Poor Caroline. She had probably fallen asleep on the sofa in her office, waiting for him to finish up tonight. Although she continued to try to hold him at bay, sometimes late in the evening like this, Nick would rouse her from slumber and succeed in getting her to make love with him. Over the passing weeks, he had got very adept at sensing when she would prove most vulnerable, most susceptible to his amorous advances. Deep down inside, he thought this was perhaps not very chivalrous of him. But when he weighed it against his desire to win her heart, he didn't care. She was his wife, and there was no way he was going to lose her.

Reaching her office, he withdrew his key to it from his pocket and unlocked the door. Ever since the incident with Paul Andersen, Nick had always insisted on her keeping it locked after 6:00 p.m. Now, as he stepped inside, he spied his wife as he had suspected he would: asleep on the couch. She looked very young—half woman, half child, he thought—curled up there beneath a hand-knitted afghan.

Crossing the floor, he bent and kissed her mouth. When Caroline stirred and smiled up at him drowsily, Nick knew—his groin tightening with desire—that he was going to get lucky again tonight.

* * *

Exiting the service elevator, the intruder sneaked down the dimly lit halls to the laboratory. As he had known it would be, it was locked up tight. But that wasn't a problem. That's what his Fortune Cosmetics identification card was for. Glancing covertly up and down the corridor, he pulled the ID card from his pocket. Turning it sideways, he inserted it into the door's locking mechanism, drawing the card's magnetic strip down the slot. On the pad, the light changed from red to green, and he pushed open the door, momentarily holding his breath, half expecting an alarm to sound. But there was nothing.

Moving swiftly inside, he made his way to Nick Valkov's office. By the glow of his flashlight, the intruder could see that the wall safe was right where it was supposed to be. He smiled, pleased. It was always a good sign when the advance information he had been given was correct. He examined the safe. It was a tough customer, but he could drill through it. Setting his gear bag down, he unzipped it, removing a conelike device that he affixed to the dial. A few minutes later, he had the dial off the safe and was unscrewing the dial ring. Then, choosing a bit intended for heavy-duty work, he inserted it into his drill and began to bore into the safe. The plate behind the dial was meant to foil burglars. He estimated it would take him at least half an hour or more to drill through it.

* * *

Caroline thought she must be the most weak-willed person alive to keep surrendering to her husband. Time and again, she had told herself she wouldn't do this. And still, it kept on happening. It was as though Nick *knew* when all her defenses would be down and she would give in to him. Even now, as his hands roamed over her naked body, she wanted him again, felt her trembling thighs open for him as though of their own volition. His palm cupped her mound, fingers playing with dark curls, sliding down the slick, fragile seam of her, thrusting deep inside her, arousing her still-throbbing body anew.

"Nick..." she breathed.

"Hmmm?" He kissed her mouth, nuzzled her throat and breasts.

"I've... told you... this has to... stop...."

"So? Stop me, then." He captured her nipple gently between his teeth, tugging on it, teasing it with his tongue. "Just say you don't want me to continue, and I won't." His thumb found the tiny nub nestled between the sensitive folds of her, began circling and rubbing it, making her arch against him involuntarily, a low moan escaping from her lips.

Caroline knew he was telling her the truth, that he would stop anytime she asked him to. The problem was that she couldn't seem to ask. Every time she opened her mouth to speak, he kissed her, his lips and tongue silencing anything she might have said, leaving her breathless and aching for him. He knew she wanted him inside her. His bronzed body moved to cover her pale one, and he pushed into her, filling her, making her gasp softly.

The rhythm he set was familiar to her now, longed for, welcomed. She wrapped her legs around his waist, taking him deep inside as he drove in and out of her, brought them both to blind, shattering fulfillment.

Afterward, they dressed, and Nick locked up her office while Caroline summoned an elevator to take them downstairs. When the car came, they stepped inside. But instead of pushing the button for the parking garage, she hit the number for her husband's floor out of what had now become habit.

"Damn!" she swore softly. "Now we'll stop at the lab. Sorry. I must be more tired than I thought."

"It's all right, baby. It's only a few minutes wasted." Nick pulled her against him, cradling her head against his shoulder and pushing the right button. "And you can sleep in the car on the way home. We'll stay at the apartment tonight."

The elevator sped downward, then lurched to a halt, the doors opening to reveal the laboratory across the hall. Without warning, Nick's strong arm shot out, preventing the doors from closing when they began to clang shut again moments later.

"What's the matter?" Caroline asked, glancing up at him, puzzled. "Did you forget something in your office?"

"No. There's somebody in the laboratory." Nick's face and voice were grim. He flicked the Stop switch on the elevator. "Caro, get on the elevator phone and call security. Then get out of this car and take the fire-escape stairs back up to your office. Lock yourself in, and don't open the door to anybody but me. Do you understand?"

"Yes, but where are you going? What are you planning to do, Nick?"

"Catch whoever's in the lab, of course."

He was gone before she could protest, jerking his identification card from his lab coat and ripping it down the slot of the locking mechanism for the laboratory door.

The intruder had finished drilling through the safe. Shining a small, high-beam light through the resulting hole, he watched the wheels moving inside as he rotated the nub of the dial until they lined up and wouldn't turn anymore. Then, taking a set of lock picks from his pocket, he inserted one into the keyhole, deftly manipulating it until he was able to throw the bolt on the safe.

"*Voilà!*" he whispered to himself, grinning. Opening the safe door, he removed the single diskette inside and tucked it into the pocket of his uniform. Then he packed his tools away into his gear bag and hoisted it over his shoulder. Outside in the laboratory, he looked around to determine what flammable chemicals were available to him. Yanking containers from shelves at random, he dumped their contents around the laboratory.

He was just preparing to strike a match to set fire to it all when, across the hall, a pair of elevator doors rolled back to reveal a man and woman inside the car.

And the man saw him.

Nick was totally unprepared for what happened when he tore open the laboratory door. Fire exploded before his eyes, blinding him and sending him staggering back, leaving him feeling as though he had been scorched. But he did not think of his own personal safety, only of that of his wife and the secret youth formula. Dimly, he heard Caroline screaming, and he realized she had disobeyed his instructions and not gone back upstairs.

Then the intruder rushed past him. A ski mask covered the intruder's face, protection against the flames and smoke sweeping through the lab. Nick chased after him, thinking only that the man mustn't get hold of Caroline, to abduct her and use her as a hostage. She would be worth a fortune in ransom—and the intruder might kill her. In the corridor beyond the laboratory, Nick tackled the man, and they both went down, grappling and rolling. The intruder tired to scrabble away, but Nick caught his ankle and dragged him back, then socked him in the jaw.

Caroline looked on, stricken, the fire alarm blasting deafeningly in her ears. Then, all of a sudden, she realized the sprinkler heads weren't functioning, that no water was coming from the ceiling to douse the flames in the laboratory. Panicked, she raced down the hall, jerking open the panel that concealed one of the fire extinguishers located on each floor. The canister was so big and heavy that she could hardly lift it, and she finally wound up dragging it down the hall to the laboratory.

Reading the instructions on the tank, trying to ignore the fact that Nick and the intruder were still locked in a vicious struggle only a few feet away, Caroline jerked the pin free and depressed the handle. Foam sprayed from the fire extinguisher, beginning to smother the flames that swept through the laboratory. Acrid smoke billowed through the air, burning her eyes and nose, leaving her coughing and gasping for air as she battled the blaze. With a sinking heart, she realized that despite the fact that she was keeping the fire at bay, her efforts weren't going to be enough to save the laboratory, that it was possible the whole of the building would wind up being set aflame.

"Nick!" she cried urgently. "Nick!"

He heard his wife screaming. A quick look at the laboratory apprised him of the danger. But the glance cost Nick his hold on the intruder. Lashing out violently with his legs, the intruder kicked Nick to one side, then scrambled to his feet and fled down the corridor before Nick could catch him. But as the intruder made his escape, the diskette he had stolen tumbled from the pocket of his uniform. He swore foully. There was no time to retrieve it. Nick was charging down the hall after him. Still cursing, the intruder barged into the fire-escape stairwell and pounded down the steps.

Letting him go, Nick picked up the diskette and stuffed it into the pocket of his lab coat. Then he ripped open another panel at the far end of the corridor and removed the fire extinguisher inside, running back to help Caroline. By now, the security personnel she had summoned earlier had arrived on the scene, along with some of the cleaning crews.

"One of you get down to the basement!" Nick shouted as he sprayed foam into the laboratory. "The intruder must have shut the water off at the main. That's why the sprinkler heads aren't working. The rest of you seal off the building. Call the police. Call Mrs. Fortune. The intruder went down the stairs."

One of the security men raced away to the basement. Two others dashed into the stairwell, while yet another yanked his cellular phone from his belt to dial 911—to be told that the fire department was already en route in response to the alarm. Some minutes later, the sprinkler system came on, dousing the blaze, much to Caroline's relief. She shut off her fire extinguisher, panting hard from her exertions.

"Caroline—sweetheart, are you all right?" Nick asked as he turned off his own cannister and set it aside before striding toward her, his brow knitted with concern. He took her in his arms. "You're not hurt?"

"No, I'm fine. Just tired."

"Thank God that's all! Why in the hell didn't you do what I told you? Damn it! That man might have kidnapped you, held you as a hostage, injured you—or worse! And if that had happened, I'd never have been able to live with myself!" Not caring who was watching, Nick kissed her fervently, letting her go only when police officers and firefighters appeared on the scene, followed by Kate and Sterling Foster.

"Nick, what happened here?" Kate queried sharply as her gaze took in the destruction in the laboratory, the police officers and firefighters taking statements from those who were present.

"An intruder. He broke into the lab and my office and tried to steal the diskette containing the equation for the secret youth formula. No, don't worry, Kate. He didn't get it. But he would have if Caro and I hadn't been here so late. He splashed around a bunch of chemicals, set the lab on fire and attempted to escape. I fought with him. But I had to let him go to help Caroline contain the blaze. Otherwise, it might have spread throughout the entire building. I'm sorry I didn't do better."

"Don't be," Kate said tersely. "You did fine. You did the right thing, Nick. If the building had burned, people might have been injured or killed. I'm just so glad that didn't happen. You saved Fabulous Face, and the lab can be rebuilt. I've got a cleanup crew on the way now. They can work through the night. Then, tomorrow, we'll have a better idea of the damage. Meanwhile, why don't you and Caroline go on home now? Caroline's barely on her feet," Kate observed, hugging her granddaughter tightly.

"I'm sorry, Grandmother." Caroline stifled a yawn.

"No, it's all right. It's late. You're exhausted, and you've had a harrowing experience. Nick, take her on home."

"Yes, I will. Come on, baby," he murmured to his wife. "Let's get you home and into bed. Good night...Grandmother."

Kate smiled, her eyes warm and kind. "Good night, Nick, Caroline. I'll see you both tomorrow."

"Grandmother?" Sterling gazed at Kate inquiringly. "What's that about?"

"That, my dear friend, is about having found the right man for my granddaughter."

"What do you mean?"

"Do you know what Nick did some days ago with the bonus money Jake paid him to marry Caroline?"

"No." Sterling shook his head. "What?"

"He put it into a trust fund for his and Caroline's children."

"You're kidding!" The attorney's mouth was agape at this news.

"Ha! Never doubt a woman's intuition, Sterling." Kate chuckled. "I told you I'd get at least two grandkids out of this deal. And I will. Now, find the detective in charge of this mess. I want whoever's responsible for this fire found and punished. Some rival cosmetics firm has somehow learned about my secret youth formula, I just know it! They're trying to steal it, and I won't have that, Sterling. Nobody gets the best of Kate Fortune. Nobody!"

Seventeen

Nick drove Caroline home to their apartment in the city. Inside, despite the lateness of the hour, they took a shower together, since they were both covered with smoke and with dried foam from the fire extinguishers. Afterward, they climbed into bed together, Nick drawing Caroline quietly into his arms, seeming to sense that she wanted just to be held close.

"I'm so worried, Nick," she said softly as she idly traced tiny circles amid the fine, dark hair on his broad chest. "After tonight, I think your suggestion that somebody made false accusations to the INS about you in order to get rid of you so you couldn't finish Grandmother's secret youth formula was right. Why else would anyone have broken into the building, into the laboratory, and tried to steal the diskette?"

"I can't think of any other reason, baby. So now I believe we *do* have to consider the possibility that some rival cosmetics firm has learned about Fabulous Face. That being the case, I'm afraid we're going to have to conduct some kind of internal investigation to find out who the spy in our midst is."

"It's so awful, Nick, to think there's a . . . a *traitor* working at Fortune Cosmetics! To wonder who or what the next target may be. What if whoever is behind this should go after Grandmother or something?"

"There's no reason to believe that'll prove true, sweetheart," he replied, stroking her hair comfortingly. "Besides, I'm sure that after tonight, we'll all be taking appropriate security measures from now on. *You* are certainly going to take them, Caroline, no matter what. We were just damned lucky that intruder didn't grab you on his way out the door. It was very brave of you to want to stay behind to try to help me, to battle the fire. But you might have been hurt or even killed. I won't have that. If necessary, I'll hire private security for you myself."

"You—you mean a—a bodyguard?"

"Yes, I do."

"Oh, Nick. Do you really believe whoever's behind all this would—would go so far as to kidnap me or a—a member of the family?" Caroline was frightened by the very thought.

"I don't know, baby. But where you're concerned, I'm just not prepared to take that chance. You're my wife. My responsibility. What kind of a husband—or a man—would I be if I let anything happen to you?" Nick didn't add how the idea of losing her tore at his heart, how stricken he had been to hear her screaming tonight, to see her so courageously fighting the fire, to think how near the intruder had been to her. Nick knew that if it had been necessary, he would have handed over the secret youth formula to save Caroline's life. But how could he tell her that, tell her that he loved her? Despite the fact that when she was in a vulnerable mood, he could now sometimes coax her into sharing his bed, she had no feelings for him beyond that. Or so he thought.

But he was wrong. Only, lying there in his embrace, Caroline didn't know what was in her husband's mind. She had heard nothing except for the word *responsibility*. It was such a little thing—but to her, it was everything, proof that no matter what she had done, how she had, much against her better judgment, more than once given in to Nick's desire for her, she still hadn't managed to win his heart. The realization dispirited her. She didn't know what else to do, what else to say.

Although she had changed her outward appearance to please him, inwardly, she was still the same. A trifle shy and insecure, uncertain where a man was concerned, thanks to how she had been used and emotionally wounded by Paul Andersen in the past. She was no femme fatale. She knew that. Maybe regardless of what her husband had said, she hadn't pleased him. Maybe he wanted her only because so long as he was married to her, there wasn't any other woman available to him.

Caroline felt she should be shamed for having so little pride in herself that she was willing to take Nick however she could get him, on whatever terms he dictated. But her love for him was such that she no longer cared.

Even worse was the fact that she had let him make love to her without either of them taking any precautions against pregnancy. Despite the fact that she had told him she wasn't on any form of birth control, it hadn't seemed to matter to him. So she thought that after their conversation about it, Nick must believe she had gone on the pill or something. Caroline felt guilty at deceiving him, but she wanted her husband's baby. Even after she and Nick got divorced, she knew now that he wasn't the kind of man who wouldn't love and be a father to his child. And she deserved something from this marriage, she thought, a part of Nick that would be hers for always, deeply loved and treasured.

"Nick, do you think Paul had anything to do with what happened tonight?" she asked softly. "He was angry about our marriage—and even madder about being fired. He must know you insisted upon it to Grandmother. He must surely blame you. Perhaps that's why the lab and the secret youth formula were targeted."

"That thought has crossed my mind, as well. That's why, in the morning, I'm going to hire a private investigator to check Andersen out. Why aren't you asleep, baby?" Idly, Nick rubbed his hand over the short, puffed sleeve of her nightgown, caressed her shoulder. "I thought you were exhausted."

"I am. But my mind is so unsettled that I can't seem to get to sleep."

"Understandable under the circumstances. Do you want a drink or something? Some hot chocolate?"

"Hmmm. That sounds nice, actually."

"Coming right up, then." Flicking on the lamp on the night table and slipping from bed, Nick padded off to make the hot chocolate, unaware of how Caroline watched him as he strode toward the kitchen. He wore a pair of burgundy silk boxer shorts—and nothing else—and she could not help but admire his tall, muscular figure, the contrast of the rich color against his bronzed skin. He returned shortly later to hand her a steaming mug.

"Oh, you even put marshmallows in it!" she exclaimed, somehow oddly touched by the gesture as she gazed down at the foamy hot chocolate. "I haven't had those in it since I was a child."

"Well, now, what's a cup of hot chocolate without marshmallows?"

"My thoughts exactly. You're a man after my own heart, Nick," she said lightly as she sipped the rich, sweet drink.

"Yes, I am, Caro," he responded just as casually—but his dark eyes smoldered intensely as he looked at her, sending a shiver of excitement and a tiny, sudden flame of hope shooting through her.

Was it possible he was actually serious? Caroline wondered. She didn't know, was too afraid of being rejected to ask, to tell him that her heart was already his.

Eighteen

The break-in, the attempted theft of the secret youth formula and the fire in the laboratory had all convinced Kate that she could not afford to wait any longer, that sending a team from Fortune Cosmetics down to the Amazon jungle would only attract further attention to Fabulous Face, alerting not only whoever had been behind the machinations against Nick and the company, but also other rivals in the marketplace. She must go herself—and go today. Jake would have to take care of things at Fortune Cosmetics in her absence, see that the laboratory was restored to its former condition and that additional security measures were enacted immediately. She had dictated a lengthy memo, detailing the steps she wanted Jake to undertake, and had copied it to Sterling. Between them, her son and her attorney could handle matters.

And when her housekeeper expressed concern, Kate ignored her, saying, "The break-in, attempted theft and fire, as unfortunate as they were, will provide a perfect cover. You may call the office this morning and inform them that I won't be in today. You may dis-

creetly suggest that as I am 'elderly—'"
Kate's voice was dry, and she scowled "—the shock to
my sensibilities was considerable, that I passed the
night poorly, and that as a result, I am resting today."

"Yes, I might can get away with that for a few days,
Miss Kate. But what then? You surely cannot think
you are going to fly down to South America, hike
through the jungle and find this undoubtedly mythi-
cal plant in less than a week!"

"No, of course not. I only need a head start. Once
I'm actually in South America and have the arrangements for my trek in place, I will cable Jake and Sterling at the office. By then, it will be too late for them
to do anything about my plans. I'll be off into the rain
forest before they can do anything to stop me."

"I still don't like it, Miss Kate," Mrs. Brant declared sternly, shaking her head. "How do we know
this is a rival cosmetics company behind all this? How
do we know it isn't that foolish Paul Andersen, bent
on revenge, for instance? How do we know who or
what is the next target? It could be you. Better for you
to stay home, hire a bodyguard. You are a rich and
famous woman. You could be a kidnapping victim.
Someone might snatch you for the secret youth formula—and you will have no protection in the jungle!"

"Yes, but nobody will be looking for me there, either. So don't worry. I'll be perfectly safe. Now, let's

get on our way to the airport. Did you call ahead, so the corporate jet will be fueled up and waiting?''

"Much against my better judgment, yes, I did."

"Good. Let's go, then."

Realizing from the determined expression on Kate's face that nothing she said or did was going to persuade her to change her mind, Mrs. Brant sighed heavily. Reluctantly she arranged for the baggage to be taken to the car. A few minutes later, Kate was en route to the airport.

"I tell you, there is something wrong." To emphasize this conclusion, Jake slammed his hand down on the Honduras-mahogany conference table in the meeting room where he had assembled Caroline, Nick and Sterling. "Mother is never ill—and while she might have been upset by the other night's events, she would *not* have taken to her bed like a helpless old woman! If anything, I'd expect her to be out prowling the city, hunting down the intruder herself."

"Dad, even though it's often hard to remember, she *is* seventy." Caroline pointed out this fact quietly— because she was worried, too. She simply couldn't recall a time when her grandmother hadn't been in her penthouse office at Fortune Cosmetics by eight in the morning.

"No, I agree with Jake," Sterling declared, his brow knitted with concern. "Even if Kate were sick, she wouldn't refuse to come to the telephone or to see any of us. Why, she and I have had dinner together at least three times a week ever since Ben died. I'm not just Kate's attorney—I'm her best friend!" The lawyer was indignant at the idea that Mrs. Brant had last night determinedly refused to open the front door of Kate's house to him.

"Jake and Sterling are right, Caro. This so-called nervous upset is just totally out of character for your grandmother," Nick insisted, patting her hand comfortingly, knowing how anxious she was about Kate's welfare. "I think one or more of us ought to drive over to her house this morning—and refuse to leave until we get some answers."

"My sentiments precisely." Jake nodded vigorously. "Mother's up to something. I'd stake my life on it! God," Jake groaned. "I hope she hasn't gone off on some wild tangent to catch the intruder. I wouldn't put it past her to be on the streets of Minneapolis right this very minute, disguised as a bag lady and pushing a shopping cart or something, questioning everybody she thinks even remotely resembles a snitch for the police!"

The reality was far worse, the four discovered, once they had driven over to Kate's house and finally managed to badger Mrs. Brant into admitting them.

"The Amazon!" Sterling cried, stricken at the news of Kate's whereabouts and abruptly sitting down on a chair, as though his legs had given out from under him.

"What do you mean Mother's traipsed off to the Amazon jungle?" Jake demanded angrily, distressed. "Why on earth would she have Bucky fly her down there in the corporate jet?" Bucky was Fortune Cosmetics' primary private pilot.

"Bucky didn't fly her, Mr. Jake. Miss Kate flew herself," Mrs. Brant announced reluctantly, knowing the further consternation this information would engender. "Believe me, I was against this trip from the very start. I did all I could to convince Miss Kate not to go. But you know how she is when she is determined on something. There was no stopping her. She was most upset by the break-in and decided she could no longer wait on Dr. Valkov to complete all his tests for the secret youth formula. She also thought that to send a team down to the Amazon rain forest would only attract unnecessary attention to Fortune Cosmetics, perhaps causing Fabulous Face to be revealed to the entire industry before it is ready for unveiling."

"So she took matters into her own hands," Nick said grimly. "Of all the foolhardy notions Kate has ever had since I've known her, this is the worst. We don't even know whether the maiden flower truly exists. I don't want to alarm anyone further, but the truth is that she may have gone off on a wild-goose chase and placed herself in unknown peril by her actions."

"What do you mean, Nick?" Caroline's face was pale with anxiety. She had been sick earlier this morning and still wasn't feeling particularly well—a delayed reaction to all that had occurred at Fortune Cosmetics the other night, she thought.

"Sweetheart, since the intruder managed to escape the other night, we don't really know who or what is behind these attacks on me and Fortune Cosmetics. So we also don't know who or what their ultimate goal may be. We can theorize that it's the secret youth formula, but we can't be sure. It could be Kate. Further, not all the South American Indian tribes are friendly. In the past, their warlike activities have run the gamut—everything from blow darts dipped in frog venom to arrows poisoned with curare. Caro, umpteen people have gone into the Amazon jungle and never come out again. An expedition like this needed to be planned and put together very carefully—not some half-baked trek arranged in a few days," Nick asserted.

"One of us will have to catch a commercial flight down to South America." That Jake was extremely upset was plain. "Sterling, I think you should be the one to go. As much as I'm worried about Mother, she would never forgive me if I went off and left Fortune Cosmetics at the moment, before I've got all the new security measures into place."

"I agree." Turning to Mrs. Brant, Sterling instructed her to call the airlines and book a flight for one to Rio de Janeiro as soon as possible. "I do have to tell you all, however, that I'm not sure how much good my going down there will do, whether or not I can pick up Kate's trail. She could be anywhere by now."

"Yes, that's true," Nick stated thoughtfully. "While you're on the phone to the airport, find out if Kate filed a flight plan. If she did, then we'll at least have some idea of her destination."

"Oh, that's a good idea, Nick," Caroline said, unaware of how she instinctively reached for her husband's hand, seeking comfort.

The past few days had seen her love for him deepen and grow even stronger. He had stepped into her family as easily as though he had always belonged, had been a part of it. And he had handled the break-in and fire in the laboratory with the ease and authority of one long accustomed to command. Now his concern for Kate's well-being was evident, and his analysis of the situation and the suggestions he had made were intelligent. She knew he had earned both her father's and Sterling's respect and admiration—something Paul Andersen had never managed to accomplish.

"Well, I guess that's all we can do here for now, so we'd better get back to the office." Jake rubbed his temples, as though he had begun to suffer a headache. "I'm sure I don't need to tell you what I think of your conduct in this matter, Mrs. Brant. I know how loyal you are to my mother, but in this instance, you should have called me."

"Yes, Mr. Jake. Perhaps you are right," the housekeeper concurred gravely. "If anything should happen to Miss Kate because I did not, I will never forgive myself."

The vast Amazon rain forest spread out beneath her in myriad shades of green bisected by the enormous, muddy river that shared the jungle's name. It was an awesome, breathtaking sight, Kate thought as she gazed out the windows of the Fortune corporate jet.

She had not pushed herself on the trip. Instead, she had made the long flight in easy stages, telling herself it was the only sensible thing to do. Even now, she didn't want to admit to herself that perhaps Mrs. Brant had been right—that she wasn't as young as she used to be.

Regardless, she was here now, and that was what counted. She would set the plane down at the airport in Rio de Janeiro, then go about putting together her expedition. Once the plans for it were finalized, she would cable Jake and Sterling. But such was her enthusiasm for this venture, the idea that at long last, Fabulous Face was truly about to become a reality, that Kate hadn't been able to resist making a quick swing over the Amazon rain forest itself first.

Confident in her security, Kate had not bothered to check the jet's interior this morning, however. So she was unaware that during the night, a hijacker had crept aboard and concealed himself at the rear of the plane. Nor was she at first cognizant of his presence as he now sneaked from his hiding place to make his way to the cockpit.

Before Kate knew what was happening, the stowaway had the muzzle of his automatic pistol jammed painfully against her temple.

"Now, listen to me very carefully, you old bat," he rasped in a hard, cold voice that sent a chill down her spine. "Because your life depends on you doing exactly what I tell you. Do you understand?"

Swallowing hard, Kate nodded mutely, determinedly reining in her fear. This must be the man who had broken into Fortune Cosmetics and set fire to the laboratory, she speculated, the man who had attempted to steal the formula for Fabulous Face. How he had got aboard, she didn't know. But one thing was for certain—he wasn't going to get the best of her, no matter what! She might be elderly, but she wasn't dead. In fact, Kate thought, her age might actually work to her advantage, as doubtless the man believed her to be frail and helpless. Well, he would soon learn his mistake!

"I want you to look around out here and find a place where you can safely land this jet," he instructed her.

"And just where do you suggest I search for such a strip?" she asked tartly. "You can see for yourself that there's very little open ground below, especially a patch large enough to handle a small corporate jet like this. I'm not flying a Piper Cub here, you know."

The gun muzzle jabbed into her skull warningly. "I've never liked redheads. So don't get smart with me, or I'll blow your damned fool head off!" the hijacker growled. "Now, land this plane, damn you!"

"Very well," Kate agreed stiffly. "That looks to be a road down there, where the natives have been slashing and burning the rain forest. I'll try to set us down there. But don't blame me if something goes wrong. This isn't a drug-running-type plane, which can land practically anywhere, and I'm not that kind of daredevil pilot, either."

"Just get us down, you old hag!" the stowaway spat out curtly.

Wordlessly, Kate maneuvered the controls of the jet so it began to descend. All the while, the wheels of her brain churned furiously. Doubtless the hijacker couldn't fly a plane. Otherwise, he wouldn't have needed her alive to land it. But once they were down, she might no longer be of any use to him—and even if she were, there wasn't any telling what he intended to do with her. She envisioned all sorts of horrors—the worst of which was being kept drugged and helpless so that she eventually degenerated into a senile old woman.

Kate decided she would rather be dead, and as the jet leveled out and started to touch down, she abruptly knocked the gun from the hijacker's grasp and, bolting from her seat, attempted to push past him. The plane bumped on the rough road—which was no more than a track, really—and bounced up again. The wings began to rock wildly, the motor to strain and whine ominously. The jet was out of control, but there was nothing Kate could do to stop it as she struggled frantically with the stowaway.

The pistol skidded across the floor of the plane, as did Kate and the hijacker. But he was younger, stronger. Catching hold of a seat, he hauled himself upright, diving for his gun. In moments, he had it pointed straight at her, and she knew he was going to shoot her. It was the last coherent thought she had before the crazy motion of the jet threw her against the door. At the impact, the door flew open without warning, and she was flung out violently.

She struck the ground, rolling over and over, feeling a sudden, sharp pain in her hip, which left her gasping and moaning. Seconds later, a giant flash blinded her as one of the wings of the plane was ripped off by a row of trees. The jet seemed to cartwheel dementedly, then it exploded, the blast deafening her and spewing debris in every direction. Something hit Kate in the head—she never knew what—and then a great cloud of blackness swirled up to engulf her.

The natives who witnessed the plane crash and found Kate's unconscious body were friendly and skilled in medicine. Laying her upon a makeshift stretcher, they carried her away to their village deep in the Amazon jungle.

Nineteen

"Caroline sweetheart, what is it? What's wrong?" Nick asked with concern as, hearing her suddenly cry out, then burst into tears, he rushed into the kitchen of their house at the lake.

Her hand trembled as she replaced the telephone receiver in its cradle, and tears streamed down her face. Blindly, she moved into the circle of his arms. "Oh, Nick! Nick!" she sobbed. "Grandmother's ... dead!"

"Dead? No, that can't be! Are you—are you sure, Caro?"

"Yes, that was Dad on the—on the phone. Sterling called ... from South America. They've located the corporate jet. Grandmother must have—must have ... developed engine trouble or something, because she was trying to—to land in the jungle. Oh, Nick, she—she crashed, and the—the plane exploded! They found her...body amid all the wreckage—or at least, what's left of it. Sterling said she—she was burned ... you know, beyond recognition. Oh, Nick!"

"Hush, baby. Hush, now. Sweetheart, I am so sorry... so very sorry. I know how much you loved your grandmother. Here, why don't I take you upstairs so you can lie down, and then I'll fix you a drink or something."

Numbly, Caroline started from the kitchen. But she was crying so hard that she couldn't see where she was going and stumbled. At that, wordlessly, Nick swept her up in his arms and carried her up the steps to his bedroom, where he laid her down on the massive canopy bed. He drew the curtains against the sun that daily grew brighter as the long winter melted into spring. Then, striding into the bathroom, he wet a washcloth and, after wringing it out, returned to place it upon Caroline's forehead. From the tea wagon in one corner of the room, he poured her a small snifter of brandy, insisting she drink it down. After that, he lay down beside her, gathering her into his embrace and massaging her head soothingly until, at long last, she finally drifted into slumber.

As Nick gazed down at his sleeping wife, his brow knitted anxiously. She had not really been well since the night of the break-in. And although she hadn't yet said anything to him, he suspected she was pregnant. He speculated that her birth control methods must have failed her and that the reason she hadn't told him was because she didn't want his baby or planned to leave him. And Nick would be damned before he would let that happen. If, to prevent it, he had to hogtie his wife and sit on her for the next nine months, he would.

Then his thoughts abruptly turned to Kate Fortune. He couldn't believe she was gone, that she hadn't somehow cheated death—she had been so vibrant, so indomitable. But there was no reason, he supposed, to doubt the identification of the body since there hadn't been anyone aboard the corporate jet with her. He wondered if the plane, as it appeared to have experienced some kind of mechanical failure, had been sabotaged. Undoubtedly, the same notion had occurred to Sterling, and he would be checking it out.

Realistically, there was nothing Nick could do to help from this end, other than to keep Caroline safe. His arms tightened around her. He would kill anybody who attempted to hurt her or their baby, he thought determinedly.

It seemed to Caroline that practically everything since the start of the new year had gone totally wrong—beginning with the INS's attempt to deport Nick. Now, hard on the heels of the news of her grandmother's death had come another letter from the INS, sternly insisting that she and Nick report to the local INS office for a formal interview and investigation into their marriage.

"What are we going to do, Nick?" she asked after he had read the missive to her.

"I don't see what else we can do, sweetheart, but keep the appointment," he replied soberly. "I mean, it's not as though either of us can afford to go into hiding. Besides which, if I actually *did* do something like run away, the INS would see to it that I never became a legal citizen of the United States. But there's no need for you to worry, Caro. The INS can't prove that our marriage is anything other than genuine. However, I'm afraid this *does* mean that we won't be able to get a divorce anytime soon." *In fact, not ever—if I have anything to say about it!* Nick thought grimly, although he didn't speak the words aloud.

"I'm...sorry," Caroline said quietly, biting her lower lip, anguished by the thought that he must be eager for them to be quit of each other. "I—I know how upsetting that must be to you, how—how much you must long to have your freedom back."

"No doubt, you feel the same," Nick answered stiffly, hurt and angered by the fact that he appeared to mean little or nothing to his wife, despite the fact that he had shared her bed and that she was doubtless carrying his child.

"Well, it isn't as though we ever believed our marriage were going to last forever." She pointed this fact out listlessly, turning away so he wouldn't see the tears that stung her eyes.

"No, it isn't," he agreed—but he spoke to an empty room. Caroline had abruptly left the kitchen and run upstairs to her bedroom.

Resolutely, Nick strode up the stairs after her. But she had gone into her bathroom, locked the door behind her and turned on the shower, so she couldn't hear him knocking, he thought. He didn't know she was running the water only to conceal the sound of her sobbing. He was beside himself, desperate to save his marriage, to hold on to the woman he loved. He glanced around the bedroom she had chosen as her own. It was part of the problem, he decided furiously. Without even thinking, he ripped open the closet door and began to yank her clothes from inside.

When Caroline reappeared sometime later, it was to find her bedroom in total disarray, her closet empty, drawers open, her garments scattered all over the place.

"Nick, what are you doing?" she cried, stunned.

"You can't go on living in this bedroom," he insisted as he gathered up another armful of her clothes to take them into his own room. "What if the INS decides to pay us a surprise visit? If they find out we have separate bedrooms, they won't believe anything we tell them. Do you want that to happen?"

"N-n-no, of course not." Caroline's heart hammered painfully in her breast. Did he intend for her to move permanently into his bed, too? she wondered.

She received her answer later that evening, when she and Nick went upstairs to retire. As she turned to head down the hall to her own bedroom, he grabbed her hand without warning and inexorably pulled her back, asking, "Where do you think you're going, baby?"

"To—to bed," she stammered nervously, both frightened and excited by the expression on her husband's bronzed visage as his glittering dark eyes raked her intently.

"Yes, you *are* going to bed, Caro. But not in there. Not anymore," he drawled, but a note of unmistakable steel underlay the silk of his low voice. Then, as though fearing she meant to protest, to argue with him, he abruptly caught her up in his arms and carried her down the hall to his own room.

Caroline's pulse raced wildly as she clung tightly to his neck. She felt like a captive of old being borne away by a handsome, determined Cossack, that Nick's Old World tendencies had somehow at last got the best of him, that he intended to ravish her. The thought was both scary and thrilling as he tossed her down onto his bed in the darkness illuminated only by the silvery moonlight streaming in through the windows, whose curtains were open. Then he deliberately closed the bedroom door and locked it.

"Get undressed, Caroline," he demanded softly, unbuttoning his shirt.

Her hands trembled with nervous anticipation as she wordlessly did as he had instructed, then folded down the covers of the bed and slipped into it, her heart now thudding so hard that she thought it would burst. She reached to draw the blankets up around her, but Nick forestalled her as, naked, he got into bed beside her, the plump mattress settling with his weight so that she slid unwittingly into his arms.

"No, don't cover yourself against me. I want to see you—all of you—while I make love to you, baby," he murmured before his mouth took hers, his tongue plunging deep, shattering her senses and compelling her surrender.

Whimpering with the desire that flamed inside her, she opened her lips pliantly and willingly to his invasion, silently offering herself up to him. Her hands tightened into fists in his thick, dark hair as she clutched him to her, wanting and needing him, loving him with all her heart. Somehow, she would make him understand that, Caroline reflected dimly in some far corner of her mind—even if she couldn't bring herself to speak the words aloud to him.

She didn't know the same thought filled Nick's own head as he kissed and caressed her fervently, as though by doing so, he could bind her to him forever.

"Your skin is so soft and delicate and pale. I love the way it feels beneath my palms," he told her as he ran his hands possessively over her body, touching, exploring, arousing her wildly. "It's mine—every inch of it. You know that, don't you, Caro?"

"Yes, Nick..." she whispered, gladdened and thrilled by his covetousness.

He cupped her breasts, pressed them high for his mouth and teeth and tongue, teasing and torturing her endlessly. Ripples of delight coursed through her entire, pulsating body as he stimulated her nipples until they were taut and flushed, twin peaks beneath his lips and hands. And, still, he lingered there, licking and sucking greedily.

Caroline felt hot and feverish, as dazed as though she had been beset by delirium. She was scarcely aware of the soft moans that emanated from her throat, of the way in which her own hands roamed restlessly over Nick's own body, tracing the hard curve of the muscles that bunched and quivered sinuously beneath her palms. She kneaded his back, his buttocks, pressed her mouth to his throat and chest. His sweat-sheened flesh tasted of salt and smelled of musk and of the Player's cigarettes he smoked; upon his breath warm against her skin was the scent of the vodka he drank—all masculine things that incited and intoxicated her.

She could feel his hard, rampant sex rubbing against her, a portent, a promise, as he nudged her thighs apart, spreading them wide for his hand that sought the soft, downy folds of her, stroking and taunting until she was burning and aching for him inside her. But he ignored her pleading mewls, the way she arched and strained against him, seeking assuagement.

"Nick, please..." she implored.

"Please, what?" he muttered huskily, kissing her mouth, her breasts, as he slipped his fingers deep inside her, only to withdraw them, spreading quicksilver heat, before he repeated the movement languorously, tantalizingly. "If there's something you want, baby, then take it."

Caroline was shocked by her own boldness and aggressiveness, but such was the state of her arousal by then that she didn't care. She pushed him onto his back and impaled herself upon him, her breath catching raggedly in her throat as she felt his potent, throbbing sex slide into her, filling her deeply and fully. His hands closed tightly on her hips. His dark eyes gleamed with triumph and satisfaction as he began to rock her against him, seeming to know instinctively just how to hold her so that each thrust was sheer torment to her, driving her wild.

She could feel the tide of sensation building inside her unbearably. Then, suddenly, it crested and broke, wave after wave of pleasure so intense that it took her breath away. She cried out, and crushing her to him, Nick abruptly rolled her over, plunging into her until his own release came just as violently, leaving him panting harshly atop her.

Afterward, he kissed her lightly on the lips, then withdrew, pulling her against him, cradling her against his chest. With one hand, he reached into the night table, shook a cigarette out from the pack of Player's inside, and lit up, exhaling a cloud of smoke into the air. He stroked Caroline's hair idly, wondering what she was thinking.

"Are you sorry I brought you in here?" he finally asked quietly.

"No." Her response was so soft that he almost didn't hear it—but he did, and his heart leaped with hope. "Are you—are you really going to keep me in here, Nick?"

"Yes." He thought she might protest then, but she didn't. Nor did she when, after taking a last drag from his cigarette and crushing it in the ashtray, he began to kiss and caress her anew, wanting her again.

It was appropriate but ironic, Caroline thought, that their formal interview with the INS had been scheduled today, on April Fool's Day. For she was surely a fool to have fallen in love with her husband and to have succumbed to him utterly. If she hadn't been pregnant before, she certainly was now—or so the test kit she had bought at the grocery store earlier this week had informed her this morning. She didn't regret the baby; she wanted it with all her heart. But she *did* despair that despite everything, Nick had yet to speak any word of love to her.

Such was the state of her inner turmoil that Caroline was totally oblivious of the admiring glances she received from several of the male employees of the INS as she and Nick made their way through the building. Her husband, however, was not—and he scowled warningly at every man who looked at her, making it clear that she was taken.

Mr. Howard and Mr. Sheffield having plainly proved easily deceived, Nick's case had been assigned to a higher-up, Mrs. Penworthy. She was a large, formidable-looking woman with her bifocals and steel-gray hair and eyes. She did not appear as though anything escaped her notice or that she would be fooled by anyone.

When Caroline and Nick entered her office, Mrs. Penworthy glanced up at them sharply, then, in tones of grand hauteur that would have rivaled Kate Fortune on her best day, instructed them to take a seat. The newlyweds sat—Nick's expression defiant, Caroline's nervous. Mrs. Penworthy opened a thick file folder and gazed down at it slowly.

"I am not going to waste time by asking the two of you the same questions you were previously asked by Mr. Howard and Mr. Sheffield," she stated coolly. "You appear to have satisfied them as to the validity of your marriage. However, you are present here today because since that time, the INS has received as-yet-unconfirmed reports that the two of you did, in fact, wed solely so Dr. Valkov could avoid being deported from the United States back to Russia. That his continued presence in this country was, in fact, so crucial to the Fortune Cosmetics company that he was paid a bonus to enter into this bogus marriage. Is that true?"

"No," Nick lied bluntly.

"Then, Dr. Valkov, perhaps you will be good enough to explain why, on your wedding day, Mrs. Valkov's father, Mr. Jacob Fortune, transferred the sum of half a million dollars into your personal bank account—a fact uncovered by the INS during its investigation of this affair.''

''If you discovered that, then you should also have learned that shortly afterward, I used that sum to establish a trust fund for my and Caroline's children, Mrs. Penworthy. The money was a gift for that purpose,'' Nick announced impassively—however untruthfully.

Hearing this, Caroline was unable to stifle a small, startled gasp. Nick hadn't taken the six-figure bonus for himself? He hadn't wanted any money for marrying her! Good heavens! she thought, the full import of his words abruptly dawning on her. *Children!* he had said. *Their* children! Mrs. Penworthy's glance seemed to pierce right through her.

''You seem surprised, Mrs. Valkov,'' the INS agent observed dryly.

''I—I am, a little,'' Caroline confessed anxiously. ''I...ah...didn't realize until now just how generous Daddy had been. Nick handles all our—our finances.''

''Mrs. Penworthy, let's forget the song-and-dance routine and cut to the chase here,'' Nick insisted, leaning forward in his chair. ''These reports you've received are an attempt, we believe, by some rival cosmetics firm to cause trouble at Fortune Cosmetics. You've undoubtedly heard about the death of Caroline's grandmother, Kate, in a tragic plane crash in South America—and I, for one, believe that death to have been caused by someone having sabotaged the corporate jet. It should be obvious to you that Caroline and I are legitimately wed—and very happily so, I might add."

"Oh, please, Mrs. Penworthy!" Caroline cried softly when the INS agent appeared to be unmoved by Nick's declaration. "I—I love my husband! Really, I do! And we're—we're going to have a baby!" She blurted out all this without thinking, driven by a terrible sense of desperation. Then, realizing what she had said, she flushed and bit her lower lip, wondering what Nick thought and wholly unable to meet his eyes in that moment.

But much to her surprise and sheer joy, he reached over and took her hand in his. "And I love my wife with all my heart, and I'm so proud and pleased about the baby that I'm going to be passing out cigars for months! If it's a girl, we're planning to name her Katherine Fortune Valkov."

"And if it's a boy?" Mrs. Penworthy inquired, glancing at Caroline for an answer.

"Alexander—Sasha—after Nick's father."

For the first time since the interview had started, the INS agent's forbidding expression softened. "Well, I don't think there's any more I have to ask either of you, then. A body would have to be blind not to see how much the two of you really *do* love each other. Please accept my apologies on behalf of the INS for troubling you. You have both satisfied me as to the validity of your marriage—and convinced me, as well, that some unknown plot against Fortune Cosmetics has been at the root of this all along. The INS shan't be bothering you again.''

Outside the INS building, Nick assisted Caroline into the Mercedes-Benz, then slid into the seat beside her, inserting the key into the ignition. But instead of starting the engine, he turned to her soberly, his dark eyes searching and filled with a strange, hopeful light.

"Caroline, did you really mean what you said in there? About loving me?''

"Yes," she confessed softly. "I *do* love you—and I'm—I'm sorry if it makes you angry, Nick, but it's really true that we're—that we're going to have a baby.''

"I know. I wasn't quite sure until this morning, but, sweetheart, even if I *weren't* a chemist, I could read the results of a test kit as well as the next man. I guess you didn't think about that when you threw it away in the trash. And I'm so happy about the baby.'' Leaning over, he laid his hand gently upon her belly. "I hope it's only the first of many—because we aren't going to be divorced, Caroline. I love you, too, and I want very much to stay your husband.''

"Oh, Nick . . .'' Her voice trailed away as he kissed her deeply, passionately.

Finally, after a long moment, stroking her hair and cradling her tenderly against his chest, he asked huskily, teasingly, "So what do you think, Mrs. Valkov? Do I get to keep my position as your husband or not?"

She smiled up at him lovingly, her heart in her eyes. "Oh, yes, Dr. Valkov. You are definitely hired—permanently!"

*   *   *   *   *

The second book in the exciting new
Fortune's Children series is

THE MILLIONAIRE AND THE COWGIRL

by *New York Times* bestselling writer
Lisa Jackson

Coming in August 1996
Only from Silhouette Books

Here's an exciting sneak preview....

The Millionaire and the Cowgirl

She hasn't changed a bit.

The thought struck Kyle Fortune deep in his gut, bringing back memories best left forgotten as he eased his foot onto the brake of the old pickup. Bugs spattered the grimy windshield, and the interior was breathless—baked by the unforgiving Wyoming sun.

Samantha Rawlings. The girl he'd left behind. A woman now. Hell, who would have thought she would be the first person he'd run into here in Nowhere, Wyoming? So his luck hadn't changed. "Damn you, Kate," he growled under his breath, as if his feisty grandmother—the woman who had arranged this little trek back to the family ranch at the base of the Tetons—could hear him, even though she was dead. That thought almost brought him to his knees.

Bald tires rolled to a stop. "God help me." In the flash, a memory long distant seared through his mind, and he saw Samantha as he had a long time ago, lying in a field of bent grass and wildflowers, her red-gold hair fanned around her face. Her body was tanned except for the most private parts, and he'd kissed her everywhere—loving her with the wild abandon of youth, never giving a thought to the future.

He hadn't seen her in over ten years, and yet his insides tightened and air already hot enough to blister the paint from the hood of his truck and bleach the color from the grass seemed to sizzle a bit more as he crossed the gravel lot.

She didn't even flick a glance in his direction. Too intent on the stubborn-looking horse on the other end of the tether she held firmly in her hands, she didn't seem to know he'd driven up. They stood eyeball-to-eyeball, a spirited mite of a flame-haired woman and a determined Appaloosa, all rippling muscles and gleaming, sweat-soaked coat.

Sam wasn't giving an inch. Mule headed as ever, Kyle decided. "You listen to me, you miserable, over-priced piece of horseflesh," she growled, barely moving her lips. "You're going to—" She stopped short as her concentration was broken by Kyle's shadow, stretching across the toes of her boots. Her eyes glanced in his direction and she audibly gasped, her fingers losing their tenacious grip. "Kyle?"

Sensing his advantage, the horse twisted his head and stripped the reins from her hands. With a triumphant whistle, he reared and pivoted, a magnificent stallion who had won again. "Hey, wait...." But the horse was gone, racing to the far end of the corral.

"Great! Just great! Now look what you made me do!"

"It's not my fault you lost control of the horse." So her tongue was as sharp as ever. It figured.

"Sure it is." Squinting against the sun, she eyed him up and down. "So the prodigal grandson has returned. What happened? Lose your Ferrari in a poker game? Take a wrong turn on your way to Europe?"

"Something like that."

"You know, Kyle, you're the last person I ever expected to see again. Ever." Hot color caressed high, sculpted cheekbones and sweat dripped from the tip of her nose.

"I guess you haven't heard."

"Heard what?"

He felt a grain of satisfaction to be the one to break the news. "Believe it or not, I'm the new owner of this place."

"You?" She stared straight into his eyes, as if checking for lies, as if she expected him to disregard the truth or stretch it to his own advantage. "*You* own the Fortune Ranch? Just you? No one else?" Was there a note of disapproval in her steady tone?

"The whole spread. You didn't know?"

She actually paled. "I—I knew that one of Kate's children or grandchildren would probably end up with... I mean, someone was bound to inherit the ranch, but I never once thought... Oh, for the love of Mike, why you?"

"Beats me."

"You're a city boy now, aren't you?" Her chin rose in defiance. "You haven't set foot here in years."

"About ten," he agreed, and saw her gaze shift away, as if she, too, didn't want to think about that last summer they'd shared. It seemed a lifetime ago, though his blood still raced a little at the sight of her. That would have to change.

"So you're here.... Why? To live?" she asked, as if she couldn't believe it.

"For the time being. There's a catch to my inheritance."

"A catch?"

"Kate left me everything with the condition that I can't sell the place or even one item of equipment until I've lived here for six months."

Six months! Kyle was going to be her neighbor for the next half year? "But you don't intend to really stay here," she said, panic chasing through her innards.

"Haven't got much choice."

There was a time when she'd hoped to see him again, had planned the day, been ready to tell him off, nail him and call him the bastard he was. But she didn't want it to happen like this, not so unexpectedly, blindsiding her when she wasn't ready.

He looked so cocky, so citified in his starched jeans, new hat, polo shirt and polished boots. He had no place here. Why couldn't he have aged poorly? Why was he trim and fit, his face more chiseled now that all trace of boyishness had disappeared? Where was the hint of a belly? The graying of his hair? The softness of a rich man who didn't have to raise a finger? Instead he was all hard angles and tight skin, slim in the waist and hips, wide across the shoulders. If anything, time had been inordinately kind to Kyle Fortune.

Tell him, Sam, tell him now! You'll never have such a golden opportunity again. For God's sake, he deserves to know that he's got a child, that he's Caitlyn's father!

SPECIAL EDITION

Stories of love and life, these powerful novels are tales that you can identify with—romances with "something special" added in!

Fall in love with the stories of authors such as **Nora Roberts, Diana Palmer, Ginna Gray** and many more of your special favorites—as well as wonderful new voices!

Special Edition brings you entertainment for the heart!

SILHOUETTE® *Desire*

Do you want...

Dangerously handsome heroes

Evocative, everlasting love stories

Sizzling and tantalizing sensuality

Incredibly sexy miniseries like **MAN OF THE MONTH**

Red-hot romance

Enticing entertainment that can't be beat!

You'll find all of this, and much *more* each and every month in **SILHOUETTE DESIRE**. Don't miss these unforgettable love stories by some of romance's hottest authors. Silhouette Desire—where your fantasies will always come true....

If you've got the time...
We've got the
INTIMATE MOMENTS

Passion. Suspense. Desire. Drama. Enter a world that's larger than life, where men and women overcome life's greatest odds for the ultimate prize: love. Nonstop excitement is closer than you think...in Silhouette Intimate Moments!

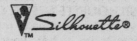

What's a single dad to do when he needs a wife by next Thursday?

Who's a confirmed bachelor to call when he finds a baby on his doorstep?

How does a plain Jane in love with her gorgeous boss get him to notice her?

From classic love stories to romantic comedies to emotional heart tuggers, Silhouette Romance offers six irresistible novels every month by some of your favorite authors!
Such as...beloved bestsellers **Diana Palmer,
Annette Broadrick, Suzanne Carey, Elizabeth August**
and **Marie Ferrarella,** to name just a few—and some sure to become favorites!

Fabulous Fathers...Bundles of Joy...Miniseries...
Months of blushing brides and convenient weddings...
Holiday celebrations... You'll find all this and much more in
Silhouette Romance—always emotional, always enjoyable,
always about love!

SR-GEN

WAYS TO UNEXPECTEDLY MEET MR. RIGHT:

♡ Go out with the sexy-sounding stranger your daughter secretly set you up with through a personal ad.

♡ RSVP yes to a wedding invitation—soon it might be your turn to say "I do!"

♡ Receive a marriage proposal by mail—from a man you've never met....

These are just a few of the unexpected ways that written communication leads to love in *Silhouette* Yours Truly.

Each month, look for two fast-paced, fun and flirtatious Yours Truly novels (with entertaining treats and sneak previews in the back pages) by some of your favorite authors—and some who are sure to become favorites.

YOURS TRULY™:
Love—when you least expect it!

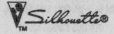